The Bloater

Also by Rosemary Tonks

NOVELS

Opium Fogs
Emir
Businessmen as Lovers
The Way Out of Berkeley Square
The Halt during the Chase

POETRY

Notes on Cafés and Bedrooms
Iliad of Broken Sentences
Bedouin of the London Evening: Collected Poems

CHILDREN'S BOOKS

On Wooden Wings: The Adventures of Webster
Wild Sea Goose

Rosemary Tonks

THE BLOATER

A NEW DIRECTIONS PAPERBOOK

Manufactured in the United States of America
First published as a New Directions Paperbook (NDP1541) in 2022
Design by Erik Rieselbach

Library of Congress Cataloging-in-Publication Data
Names: Tonks, Rosemary, author.
Title: The bloater / Rosemary Tonks.
Description: New York : New Directions Publishing Corporation, 2022.
| Series: A New Directions paperbook ; 1541
Identifiers: LCCN 2022028040 | ISBN 9780811234566 (paperback) |
ISBN 9780811234573 (ebook)
Subjects: LCGFT: Novels.
Classification: LCC PR6070.05 B58 2022 |
DDC 823/.914—dc23/eng/20220622
LC record available at https://lccn.loc.gov/2022028040

2 4 6 8 9 7 5 3 1

New Directions Books are published for James Laughlin
by New Directions Publishing Corporation
80 Eighth Avenue, New York 10011

The Bloater

I

"Hullo."

This is Fritz coming into the darkened hall, and calling out uncertainly. He says that "Hullo" more or less to himself; sometimes, if I'm there, I answer after a long half-minute: "Yes! I'm coming down." The point is that it's a quarter past two in the afternoon and I've just thrown myself down on the bed with a form of tiredness which is like drunkenness; your head goes on reeling, and there are varied layers of brand-new tiredness inside the massive, overall exhaustion, so that you go on falling through one after another. If you lie there long enough you reach the bottom, the ocean floor. Once deep down there, flat out in the pitch darkness, half buried in your bed and your thoughts … once down there, someone calls out "Hullo" with German-sounding syllables, and you *instantly* take an extra half-minute of darkness and oblivion, before letting yourself drift up to the surface and calling out, just as you hit the surface, in a voice of authority, with a sparkle in it like Asti Spumante: "All right! I'm coming."

I know perfectly well he'll go on standing there if I don't answer. He likes to register the atmosphere with his head bent a little, listening in case there are surprises in the way of people or objects. Also, he sniffs the house to see what I've been up to. If it's got a dried-up smell, like old twigs, he

thinks: "Oh, she's been working. We'll have to call an ambulance." If there's a whiff of scent—I've got a little bottle
of light brown scent which only lasts twenty minutes on the
skin, but will stay on my coat in the hall for two days—he
thinks: "Parties! Just my luck to be a poor student, while
others are going out getting sex, life, and heaven knows
what." Very, very occasionally there's a smell of silicone
polish which has been put on by me, in which case he pre-
tends to be hurt: "You want to take my job away? That's
no good. The matter is that you are taking my work." In
any case you can't please him; everything I do is to him
disgraceful, fascinating. He has very strong views about
women, they can never win: "They will get hits." In reality
he is kind, long-suffering, just, and good-natured.

Today there's a smell of polish. But Fritz could never
guess the reason for it, and I don't think I could tell him,
not without exploding with laughter. The polish went on
that little African stool in the sitting-room—not because I
look after it with care—in fact I only polished the top of
it. It went on because a huge man was sitting on the sofa
with his legs stuck out half-way across the room. This huge,
tame, exotic man was reading a book as though he was sitting in an airport lounge, with no more regard for me than
one has for the factotum in tinted nylon uniform-pyjamas
who brings a cup of coffee and wipes over the simulated
marble formica with a morsel of rubber skin. Not content
with ignoring me, this loafer, this self-regarding bloater—
smells. Oh yes, he does. I, personally, can smell him from
the kitchen door. I'm not interested in finding excuses for
him; I do see that he is large and that washing takes time, I
do see that he spends most of his life travelling, or appear-
ing in a professional capacity (he's a singer, a baritone).
Even so, it's monstrous of him. In addition to all this, he

irritates me more than any man I have ever met. There are times when he turns up, bearing some sort of gift (this only makes me angrier), and follows me to and fro "helping." I've got a feeling that bed-making is his speciality. The only time I've ever seen him *hurry* is in the direction of a bedroom. The bed I'm making up is usually for him, when he spends the night with us. And until the moment he enters it, the bedroom is only a very ordinary room with a bed in it. Then suddenly—snap pool! It's a boudoir, it's a dangerous liaison, it's the fourth floor of a Lisbon brothel, it's Madame de Pompadour and Louis XV all over again in some unaired voluptuary's den (the horrible Bourbon temperament etc.) before she gave the affair style and order.

This man wanders along the side of the bed, still carrying his despatch-case and wet umbrella, while I tuck in the blankets and snap at him. Sometimes I'm flooded with a diabolical strength and feel almost capable of throwing him out of the window, despatch-case, umbrella, reading book, voice, ego and all. I think he feels this, but instead of staggering back when he senses my flood of malice, he goes on smiling. He laps it up. And the room becomes more of a bedroom than ever.

The polish was simply another piece of self-protective malice. (He throws all my evil qualities into relief, and I'm perpetually convulsed with hysteria at my own actions, which become more and more outrageous.) I went into the kitchen and took up the tin; you open it with that old-fashioned screw at the side. The wax is mauve, slippery, fragrant. It smells as good as fresh white gum oozing out of a tree of rosin. I found a polishing rag, and with these two rough objects I was ready for him. He was still sitting there (he has a way of watching me with the whites of his eyes, and without moving) and the stool had been pitched off-centre by the thrust of his legs. The curious thing is that he never shows any sign of surprise. Anyone else, surely, would have been uneasy to see a woman with set lips enter the room, kneel down and polish away remorselessly at a stool? and this was at about six-thirty in the evening. I think he gave me a glance, as a concession to our relationship, and then simply went on reading. Exactly as though it was fit and proper for me to go about my lowly household tasks, while he rested his baritone on the sofa! You see what sort of a man he is. Still, the room smelt much better by the time I'd finished; and I had taken a limited form of vengeance on him. I know how painters feel when they refer in a special tone of voice to their "sitters"; there's always bad feeling against the one who "sits," a grudge builds up.

Impossible to explain all this to Fritz, about my exotic bloater, who smells like a bloater and has to be cancelled out with silicone polish. He *is* exotic in spite of all this. There's a loose red silk handkerchief with green spots which falls out of his top pocket, and a tie which matches and is silkily knotted just off to the left, under the wing of the collar—for the top button of the shirt has gone (or been wrenched off) and you can see the throat down to its roots and the beginning of the gigantic white marble slab of his chest. (How it stays white is a mystery.) This throat is not unattractive, and it contains his great prize—the cause of the overbearing arrogance in his step—his voice. I haven't actually heard it, because even the least sound from him, anything like an exhaust pipe humming, makes me stiffen up. And for once, he's noticed this and has the sense to keep quiet. I imagine he could reverberate like an organ pipe, and if he held low "C" in the sitting-room the claustrophobia would be unbearable. As it is the reading, and the sitting, and the whites of the eyes are more than enough.

Fritz says:

"The matter is that you have been polishing, and doing things and that is not good."

"Don't be silly. I saved up the downstairs lavatory for you, so you can look forward to that. Don't tell me I'm not generous, Fritz. How are you by the way?"

"Oh, not too bad. We are doing *Othello* at school (he means the language school), and I am to write on his wife, you know, Des—"

"Desdemona. Not so easy in a foreign language."

"You have to say what kind of woman is this Desdemona, and you know she is not so good."

"Oh Fritz! Not again. Please don't have such a down on women. Just because you had one bad love affair."

"It's not a case of that. I tell you, you find them out. They are just animals these women. I was with a girl the other night, and you know she was going on and on," he has gone very black in the face, and is holding the hammer-headed bit of the vacuum cleaner, "and I said: 'Why not?' And she would not, you know, she just turns around and says: 'No.'"

"And why shouldn't she for God's sake?"

"Because she goes on and on, that is the matter. She goes on too far, and then it's too late, and then she wants to stop."

"Well, why don't *you* stop, Fritz?"

"Because man is the hunter, that is why. The woman knows, she knows when it is the time to stop."

"What! You're telling me a little girl of seventeen with no experience knows better than you, the great Fritz, an experienced seducer of women!"

He begins to laugh, he has a very helpless, infectious laugh. After all he's twenty-two and everything is more or less amusing. He only puts on his black face for women, religion and politics. He has no idea that he is one of the most moral, most courteous people I have ever met. He is still determined to justify himself in the case of the girl who "went on."

"They *know*," he says, with the primitive vigour of a secret Bible-reader escaping from an age of psychoanalysis. "It's built into them right from the beginning."

"Oh Fritz! I never heard anything so selfish. You know what, you're picking up the morality of the pavements and finding it very convenient. Now do stop it. It's not natural to you. You're going against your nature, and it doesn't suit you. Listen, if you're so tough, do you want to take some of the rugs outside and beat them?"

He agrees. We carry out soft, dusty Persian rugs where they make an amber vapour half way down the sunlight on the little back lawn. Fritz enjoys carrying out specific tasks, and likes to have his briefing in advance like an officer at the front. Then he bites on his pipe, and fulfils the mission down to the last word. It's true he's also vague, and will leave pieces of furniture stranded out in the middle of a room, but that's only because once cleaned, they have no reality for him, and he gets dazed when it comes to arranging a room. You have to wheel the heavy chairs back into their predestined positions, and just twist a jug round, or ease a rug back on to its seabed. It's much better, even so, than having someone who forcibly arranges things for you, so that everything in the house is somehow running against the grain.

I'm not going to the electronic studio this afternoon. I'm supposed to be preparing my tapes for tomorrow. In reality, I shan't do a thing. I'll have tea with Fritz and we'll talk about communism, the good idea that went wrong. After communism, he drives the vacuum down the first-floor passage making it snarl on the wooden boards on either side of the runner, and pushing it up into corners where it moans and raises its voice. When I can't stand it any longer, I come half-way upstairs and put on a desperate face, and make overlarge gestures: "*Please*, Fritz."

He can't hear me coming on account of the din he's making, and gives a start and touches his heart (in the wrong place).

"Meintamotter" (that's what it sounds like), "I've got to finish this piece."

I swear to stick to women, and keep off communism in the future; but one forgets and gets careless and interested.

Right. I'll do some keep-fit exercises if he's going to win all his political arguments with a vacuum cleaner. The tape recorder lives on the floor under the light-switch, because that was where the delivery man put it. I suppose it could be built into a cupboard, or engrossed into some sort of mahogany unit—but meanwhile my life would slip away. I play with it expertly, switching on and off with my feet, pleased to think I'm still a monkey. Brahms is good for exercising, if you're not in love; if you are in love of course, you will simply swoon off after the first knees bend. Beethoven has too many ups and downs, the music gets awkward and thrilling, and you strain your back and make grandiose plans which waste your brain for several hours afterwards. Mozart is ideal, sane and elegant, he's not going to push you over the top—except with a fingertip, and then he'll pick you up directly you start falling. It's like exercising inside a watch, inside a piano.

Poof! How hot it is. My heart thuds away. I lock the door and strip down. The front bell rings. Fritz, who has switched off the vacuum defeated by my music, at once snaps it on again. Isn't he insufferable! (Never shall I mention Marx again in this house.) I throw on my clothes, an Aertex shirt always crumpled, and a pair of denim trousers cut as if for the Chinese Merchant Navy. Fashionable from the hips down at least, I go to the door.

It's Claudio, my good friend. Infallibly attracted by noise, by two people laughing, by sunshine, intrigue, practical jokes, anything that smacks of a good time when he can take both his feet off the ground and drift, laughing heartily over the bad parts of life without once coming down to earth, he's come to call. I've never worked out whether he's a good or a bad influence on me; and now it's too late because I'm devoted to him. He's about sixty, with a brick-red pair of cheeks decorated by side-whiskers of thick light-blue wool. He has property, knows everything, and occasionally tells me near-truths about myself. He's a terrible ally since he enters into the part assigned to him, and plays it up to the hilt—so that you have to go up and stop him, and tell him firmly when it's all over. In many ways he's like Fritz, except that he adores women, and instead of giving them "hits" he speaks of stroking their hair very gently. This may be a conversational euphemism, and I shall never know (although he talks about it perpetually) whether he has loved, or whether, when he did, he was the knowledgeable, resourceful, instinctive and improvisatory lover of genius he would have me believe. Sometimes I feel doubtful; I can imagine him wasting a good deal of time gazing and looking sloppy. But today he's Napoleon, he has his right hand stuck into the left side of his morning-suit, and is looking about for the French Army. (I said he was like Fritz.)

I open the door wide, and smile at him. He's rather surprised at this warm welcome, but hurries in anyway. And noting my clothes, and that I am panting, and have no shoes on, he looks suspicious.

"What is going on here? My God, what is she doing?"

II

By now he's looking round the hall to see if there are any signs of a strange male presence. Fritz's jacket is hidden away in the cupboard, and I'm still smiling with a horrible sweetness which should warn him that he's heading the wrong way.

"Claudi, I'm absolutely desperate."

"Are you, my dear?" He dilutes his gaze so as to make it somewhat watery and impersonal; that is, absolutely ideal for confidences. ("If I'm too eager, I shan't get a word out of her.")

"Yes, can't you *see* that I am?"

Fritz drops one of the vacuum heads upstairs, and Claudi raises his eyes to the cornice and waits patiently. At last, when nothing else happens, he risks losing the next few bumps, and says in wheedling tones:

"What is it then, darling?"

"Th*ing* is trying to come to stay again. I'll go mad."

"Who is coming?"

"My bloater, the black cloud—don't you remember, I went to the front door once and couldn't see anything at all? Because he was filling it up right to the lintel. And, Claudi" (I'm really beginning to get agitated), "if you could only hear him say '*Umm?*' on the telephone! I tell you it would drive you stark staring mad. You say something to him, and then you wait about ten minutes, and then he looks up and says '*Umm?*' I can't stand it."

He understands instantly, and courteously bites his lips.

"Yes, of course, that is terrible."

"He wakes me up because he creeps about the house in his socks so as not to disturb me. Consequently we all have to get up at about seven and do the can-can, or we might as well, if you know what I mean, darling. Last time I put a note under his door *forbidding* him to leave his room until nine o'clock."

"And what did he do?"

"He was terribly silent. Two months later he told me he'd missed a master class with a famous singer which he'd come up for specially."

"That was very naughty of you, Min."

"Is it my fault if the bogus monster insists on singing!"

"Yes, but you've got George here to help you, darling. You must make a little plan so that this fellow, this chap, doesn't come again."

George is the man I'm married to. He is much loved by everyone who knows him, and is always on the way to or from the British Museum. He pays the bills, is genuinely fond of me, and, I suspect, leads two or three lives once away from the house. Officially he is the Keeper of unprinted books at the Museum. He and the Bloater have been getting on very well just lately, laughing together over a late-night Hine's Antique in the sitting-room. George himself has a tendency to say "Umm?" but it's nowhere near so well developed as the Bloater's, he hasn't got the larynx for it and the top button of his shirt is always done up. I know quite well he can't, or won't, lift a finger in the present situation. Besides, the Bloater is *my* Bloater—Ah, so that's my secret! He's mine, and so I alone can abuse him. It's my job to make him suffer, and although I'm prepared to go into partnership with Claudi, I shan't breathe a word to George. I know perfectly well what I'm up to.

Claudi has meanwhile taken up two or three attitudes in the sitting-room. He sits down and positions his knees. Then he gets up and takes two strides, and gives his tie a going-over. Of course the morning dress! I'd almost forgotten.

"You know, you're looking very smart got up like that. Have you come to see me married at last?"

"Yes, my dear. These are my old legal trousers and this is my old legal tie."

"And your head's very handsome too, today. It's a really beautiful old legal head."

"Thank you, my dear." Although Claudi has this "my dear" tic, he always refreshes it by giving it a different twist, derisive, or tolerant, or menacing.

Now that I've paid him a half-compliment, I want something for myself.

"By the way, do you think I'm good-looking?"

"Yes, I have always felt that you were a very attractive woman." When he says "attractive" his tongue stumbles as if going over a lot of furniture: "a-ttt-ra-c-tive."

"Hmm. I don't like that word 'felt.' It's in the past tense to begin with. And you might make your response more visual in future. By the way, do stop pointing." Claudi is pointing towards the reverberations coming through the ceiling. "Your fingernails are filthy. I hope you're not going to claw at the bride with those dirty fingernails."

"I can't help having dirty fingernails. I'm a gardener, and it's absolutely impossible to keep them clean. No, I am not going near the bride. I have no wish to get into contact with her." He bows slightly, as if warding off an over-sexed bride. "By the way, did I tell you the story of the little boy who said in a sharp, brilliantly clear voice in the middle of the service: 'Mummy, when does he give her the seeds?'"

"There's a great deal too much seed-giving at the moment, due to these Penguin text-books on half-digested Freud."

"Oh! Oh! Listen to the little puritan speaking. With, goodness knows what going on upstairs. Yes, all right, we get one seed from each man of affairs, and then we get George Brown to bless it, and Barbara Castle to infiltrate it."

He's begun to play and dance about in his wedding gear. I must say it's catching, and I throw out:

"Don't forget that for chemistry you need a bunsen burner."

"Oh, go away! Now she wants a bunsen burner!"

He stops laughing suddenly, as if someone had pulled down a shutter on the shop inside his head.

"Now how am I going to find Cadogan Street?"

"I'll look it up for you." I'm already going through the A to Z guidebook, with its infinitesimal words and page 63, the favourite part of London, all yellow spots and on the point of falling out. "Here it is. You go down Sloane Street and then turn right."

"Oh yes, there's a bit of greenery and then I turn right. But where am I going to park?" He's woebegone again, and biting on the bullet.

"Enjoy yourself. You're not going to the guillotine. Listen, you'll get drunk at the reception and find yourself a nice pink and white woman, you know you will."

"No, I shan't. They're all old women, like me. I'll end up with some lousy little old woman. Oh dear. Really sometimes I wish to God there was some way out of it quickly. (He means life.) All my friends are dying or just getting more and more boring, so that I can't talk to them any more."

"Poor Claudi. Shall we have tea at the Ritz together in September?"

"Oh sweetie-pie! What a good idea! I've wanted to do that for years. Do you know, I've never been in any of the big hotels, the Dorchester, the Savoy, Claridge's? And I don't care a damn."

"But it's lovely at the Ritz because its Proustian."

2

Going along one of those dim brown corridors which lead to the electronic sound worskhop, I meet a musician I know. We have, in passing, one of those exchanges which have taken the place of comments on the weather:

"Hullo, Ron. How are you?"

"Oh, sexually frustrated as usual."

Inside the workshop no one moves. The walls are blocked in solidly with machinery, and there are free-standing machines on wheels. The light is so bright you don't even look ugly. You simply look like yourself. Fred is brooding over a little piece of paper. Jenny is sitting in front of a dashboard of dials and switches. Today she is very got-up; a tight, sexy green jersey, a leather skirt in a very elegant brown with scruffy patches to prove it's real, things on her wrists which she shakes about too quickly for me to focus, and black hair combed down on to her shoulders and then fixed in position with sparkling glue sprayed on. Possibly this is why Fred is a bit glum. When Jenny is hunting, her tea-break is a thirty-minute phone-call and her lunch-hour is *interminable*. I am very dashed by this long blue-black hair, and the corners of my mouth go down. I can just hear Claudi saying: "My God, I would die for that blue-black hair!"

Jenny looks up but doesn't smile too much because she's only half made-up, and wants to hold her face more or less immobile until the evenings when she puts on the other half. Inside this armour she's amusing, temperamental, and clever.

There's no air in the workshop, we're sealed in like tinned shepherd's pie. The clock is silent but the hands go round fast with that railway station stutter. I'm late of course, and the little silver music-stand has been put out for me already. I arrange my papers; I stop being human. There's no time to make mistakes in here, they're too expensive. We are setting a poem about Orestes to electronic sound. We're taking the sentiment straight, no wit, no discords. We know that however well we succeed, fifty "experts" (people who acquire theoretical knowledge without using it) will pour cold water on the result. And then five years later, grudgingly, and ten years later, publicly, stuff our work into the sound archives, and refer to it incessantly to intimidate future electronic composers.

Everyone is temperamental today; we skirmish. Fred has one of his "dirty sound" days on, he hears "dirty sound" every time we play anything, and we have to stop while he cleans it up on one of his machines. Now we are putting a piece of voice in. We listen. A hammy male voice croons out some dishwash. Everyone shudders; in here the wrong sort of voice is not simply an error in taste, it's grotesque.

"Try some bass cut," says Jenny.

A machine cuts off the bass notes, and a crazy high-pitched dwarf gives us the same dishwash. I always laugh, and am put in my place by a movement of silver irritation from one of Jenny's wrists (my God, Claudi!).

"Top cut," says Fred sharply.

This time the treble is expertly removed, some echo is added, and the voice is twice as hammy as before but somehow convincing. Obviously it's no good being slightly vulgar; you must be *absolutely* vulgar. Taste in the arts and theatre should never be confused with "good taste," which is static and middle-class. It's evident that we're treating this voice like a loaf of bread, first the crust off, then the foot, and now we're going to cut it into slices ... with any luck. Ah, no—Jenny is sagging.

"Jenny!"

"I'm thirsty."

"Well, have a glass of water."

"For *tea*."

She moves listlessly. Good heavens, the way her strength leaves her is a reproach to the Creator. A moment ago she was snapping switches on and off, now she can hardly press down on that little black lever which brings up the mains electricity.

"Didn't you get any sleep last night?" I'm trying to find out whether she has a hangover, so as to decide which tack to try out.

"Oh yes. Slept like a log."

Now it's my turn to sag:

"Oh God, how lucky can you be? I had insomnia. I did a Hatha Yoga exercise, drank iced water, read *War and Peace*, everything."

"Really? I had a marvellous sleep. I went straight off in the middle of a bar of Janacek's Sinfonietta (affected bitch), and slept *so* deeply, I hardly turned over. I didn't even bother to dream I was so sound asleep."

An icy depression hits me. Have you noticed when you're going through a patch of insomnia, how other people go on describing their sleep, their voices vibrating with strength?

"And I woke up in such a comfortable position, I can't imagine how I ever got into it."

Oh well, that should be good for another hour's work at least. I never heard anything so complacent. She's sitting there as though she's just laid an egg. And I fully intend to take advantage of it. We work meticulously; I boil up into little rages at my music-stand to keep them interested. I have to do this every time I want to use "feedback" or overlapping; these are considered my weaknesses and I'm forced to take the witness box and argue for them.

"But, Fred, it's just perfect there, to have a breathy voice calling 'Orestes' into the distance."

"Well yes, but you've just had this dark voice on feedback calling 'Orestes' into the distance. You're rather laying it on, you know."

"This isn't the kindergarten. These are grown-up passions. You can't lay it on enough. People feel these things."

"Do they? I don't."

If I say: "That's not fair," I shall lose the last shred of authority, and work will instantly pack up for the morning.

I'm silent. Jenny just blazes away with her eyes; I forget the wash of those sea-green eyes. But I can tell you that after a good night's sleep they're scorching. I decide to revert to a child's method of coaxing; advertisers do it when they say "if not satisfied, we promise to replace the goods," i.e. *never*, you can drop in your tracks wearing our galoshes. I give every appearance of thinking over carefully what Fred has just said; he waits moon-like and contented. When I see that he's "safe" again and has begun to chew the cud, I say:

"Hmm. I see what you mean. You may be right. Look, we'll just give it one try on feedback, and if it's totally wrong, I'll follow your judgement, and we'll take it out," i.e. never.

He knows he's whipped, but apart from telling me I'm a low cur, there's not much he can do. Suddenly I become self-righteous. Why should I have to fight for a miserable piece of feedback like this? It's unbearable. Anyone would think I was getting a gold wristwatch. Who wants to pour their life away arguing about feedback, when they could be staggering away from Harrods, loaded up and *kept*? Directly the feedback is played in, I say with a breezy quarter-deck air, looking calmly into my sailors' faces:

"I like it. Let's keep it in." Smile, smile.

They are astounded, thrown into confusion. Jenny has forgotten her half made-up face, and is eating bits of her fingers and really concentrating. Fred has retreated inside himself, and become a salaried employee who is just doing a job. I stay haughty for about two minutes. Mutiny is held off. We go on until lunch-time.

Freedom! Jenny and myself, out in the street, are looking for a new pub. The daylight is so white after the studio lights, also it's not just up in the sky, it's equal everywhere, down in behind the dustbins and round every parked car. We look at one another carefully; not too bad. She imagines that her beautiful green eyes will distract my attention from her face—what a hope! I give her my profile and hope for the best.

We need a new pub, something seedy, because Jenny wants to talk about her life in secrecy. Here's one. A battered wooden corner, like the corner of an old chest, white glass with whiter glass writing on it, and that famous tobacco-London interior light, the colour of beer itself. We order "stingos"; brown ink.

"He plays the guitar."

"Oh then you're bound to suffer, Jenny."

"It's fifty-fifty at the moment. But I'm falling in deeper and deeper. And in the beginning I never even noticed him."

"I've heard that before. It's a fatal way to start. You can't remember what you felt in the very beginning."

"Exactly! If only I could go back and have a good look at him without feeling the feelings I've got now."

"Probably wouldn't have them."

"If only he hadn't got such a marvellous sense of timing!"

"If only, if only! You must deal with the present."

We are eating harsh cheese sandwiches. The cheese itself is like crumbled masonry, and makes your gums smart. This meal is so indigestible that by four o'clock we shall be dull, wrecked. Add to that the fact that we are laughing all the time, and then gasping for air. Jenny is the one who never for an instant forgets to be feminine. I keep making mistakes, and most of my gestures are boyish. But *she* has her black hair arranged, and her arms really delicately propped up round her, so as to form a centre, a net, inside which a guitar and its guitarist might flounder about helplessly. I say:

"I can't understand you. Musicians are usually so narcissistic, they're simply not worth the candle."

She agrees noisily from the bread and cheese, biting and scoffing.

"You're absolutely right. They're beastly. But you know he came back after the party was over, and everyone else had gone home, and rang the bell—"

"What cheek!"

"That's what I said. He said something about helping me clear up. And I hadn't even focused his features then. Then he lay down on the sitting-room floor and talked in snatches about his life and ideas."

"I'm always suspicious when a man gets down on to the floor like that. I think it's a sure sign of a late developer: 'please I'm still an undergraduate, and I want to go on being unstable as long as possible.' Was he boring?"

"Not terribly. I liked the way he talked, just like a woman. Intense and jolted. Then he came and lay across my foot."

"What a good idea!"

"Wasn't it! And you know how vulnerable one's feet are. Well, here was this nice clean, thick, warm stomach lying across my foot—I forgot to mention he's got fabulous fair skin—"

"Oh! I'm beginning to enjoy these sandwiches even."

"After that I kept very still while I decided whether to put him off or not. Taking it all in all, the intelligent Cambridge commercialism of the talk, the muscular prostrate body, the dark head carefully turned away so as not to alarm me with any random thoughts—taking it all in all, I decided to sit in for the last act."

"You could always get up and ring a bell if you didn't like it."

"Well, it was most elegantly tense. And after the non-looking period, we both had a jolly good look at one another. But of course by then I was so attracted I couldn't see a thing."

"So you still don't know what he looks like!"

"Even then he *didn't move in.*"

"I say! He's really promising." I stare at her admiringly.

"That's what I thought. It was the best looking period I've ever had. First we looked hard, and then we looked restfully."

(I'm beginning to feel jealous; do I really hate the Bloater?)

"And then?"

"Then, my dear," her face is brilliantly over-excited, is she going to cheat me out of the finale? No, her eyes have wandered back to the guitarist: "Then, without any haste, and at the precise moment when I'd decided to move and

get up, he leant over slowly and kissed with the most horrible, exquisite, stunning skill—"

"Born of nights and nights and nights of helping people
clear up after parties."

"His mouth, which was the softest thing I've ever felt,
was just slightly open. He *knows everything*."

"Stop!" I'm agitated. She's gone too far, and is forcing
me to live her life. Where are my coat, my ideas, my name?
Stop, stop; it's only the lunch-hour. That barley wine was
an idiotic idea. She makes me feel I've got to justify myself;
catch the first plane to New York, or something equally
stupid. I've lost game, set, and match. "He *knows everything*." Oh! I know *exactly* what she means; and yet, what
on earth does she mean? And how does *she* know these
things? Why do the only men I know carry wet umbrellas
and say "Umm?" I'm being starved alive. Quick: the first
bookshop for a copy of the *Kama-Sutra*. I say sharply, envy
really shooting out:

"Have you got your copy of the *Kama Sutra*?"

"Have I—?" She gets the message, and damps down the
green forest fire in her eyes. It only takes her a second to
touch the necessary lever and change her mood; sophisticated young women hate to think they've gone too far in
conversation. They'll backtrack for hours afterwards, and
try to get inside your head and live down that piece of
off-the-cuff behaviour. Basically I've double-crosssed her
emotionally, but she'll forgive me because my motive is
pure jealousy. Here we go, purring together. She starts:

"But of course, my dear! That famous shiny yellow pa-
perback!"

"And the couple on it, both with eyes firmly closed."

"It's the sleeping sexness."

"I don't think anything's going on at all."

"I do."

"It's like reading a long, boring article in The *Times* right through, just because you've seen the word 'brothel' two-thirds down it. You read and read like one possessed."

"I don't think I've ever seen the word 'brothel' in Th*e Times*."

"They put it in the small print." If I let her, she would trounce me today. And I shall *have* to hear the next instalment on that guitarist, that after-party Orpheus. One last morsel of information is coming my way as we climb down from the stools. Jenny glances at her own well-bitten but not unpleasant little hand ...

"... Min, on his playing hand, he's got these long fingernails. They have to keep them long. I can't decide whether I like it or not. It's sinister, but slightly thrilling." She shudders publicly.

"Well, even if you don't know what he looks like, you can always recognise him in the dark by his long fingernails."

Our friendship is definitely rocking about, but we seem to be laughing. Outside more lightning-white daylight, and a fresh pavement breeze, one of those September breezes that begin to blow in August. We're tipsy, and I badly need a telephone box; I catch these loose habits from Jenny and pull off all sorts of emotional *coups* under her demoralising influence.

Yes, I do know someone else apart from the two umbrellas. There's Billy whom I've got to know really well, without ever being too attracted by him. We're always talking, or writing notes to one another, and it's a perfect anaesthetic. We plunge straight into essentials. If it's music, we tear apart the latest *Turandot*, and simply get roaring drunk on it all over again. This sounds as if we shout a bit at one another. Not at all. Billy hardly raises his voice, he's exact, contemporary, very masculine and controlled. He looks after himself perhaps a little too well: saunas, polished teeth, shiny shoes, champagne at all the three moments in the day when it's possible. He's vigorous, a musicologist, an all-rounder, and not too important to be rung up when I feel like it. I ring him up.

"And, Billy, she makes me feel I ought to go straight to bed with the Bloater!"

Billy never laughs at a remark like that. He knows how serious it is. He considers his reply, which is really a piece of fine dentistry—I mean he stops up all my aches and pains with steady, informative comparisons from his own life.

"I don't see why. I don't think one should ever go to bed with someone who bores one in a restaurant."

"How wise. Of course one shouldn't. How did you know he was awful in a restaurant?"

"I suppose I just sensed it. You've been out with him several times, haven't you?"

"Oh God yes. I knew his wine list routine better than my own. He'll make the same gesture for the umpteenth time while reading it—and, you know something funny? I've grown fond of that gesture while remaining irritated by it."

"Women don't like waiting when a man is ordering. It irritates them very much."

Billy is really helpful; I've instantly found a hundred reasons for damning the Bloater. I mutter it all hurriedly into the receiver:

"He'll finish the whole list, reading slowly, Billy, and the waiter will say: 'Yes, sir?' And *at last*, he'll say in an off-putting voice—as though avoiding an oral examination: 'Oh, I don't know.' And then *finally*, Billy, turning away with a helpless sort of gesture, he'll mutter: 'I suppose we'd better try No. 44.' Now I've said all this it sounds rather endearing."

"No, it doesn't."

I'm very grateful to him for not finding it endearing; because Jenny (who has gone back to the studio with a light step) would have found it so. She is riding high today, and that guitarist is probably only three down in a perfect stack of possibles. At the thought of this I ask the telephone in a low mournful voice:

"Am I getting left out of things?"

It replies with gentle decency: "No, I don't think so. One doesn't want the wrong things and the wrong people. The main trick in life is to stay well away from those. You're formed by the company you keep, you know. Let's have dinner out together on Thursday if George is working."

"I'd love to. I feel as though I've just got away from a terrible danger."

"I do hope he's not as attractive as that."

3

Mens sana in corpore sano.

That's the sub-title of the book I'm reading; I stole it out of my grandmother's house years ago, and it's called The *Cheerful Home Doctor.* I'm reading it because I'm ill in bed, struck down in the prime of life by the new welfare state disease: gout.

Gout! High living, paté, port? Well, certainly paté. But those barley-wine lunches near the electronic sound work-shop are really to blame; and George coming home and being very nasty last night. Something must have gone wrong in one of his two or three lives; or possibly he hasn't been getting enough attention from me just lately. Anyway he was sour and brooding, fingered things, and wouldn't "come round." I saw that it was useless doing amusing things, so I went upstairs, and then felt sorry by the time I reached the landing, and came down again and apolo-gised—for absolutely nothing! And George listened care-fully to my little violin tune, and then said sententiously: Well, you were a little bit inconsiderate." He has no sense of fair play. I put down the cardboard box of tissues I was carrying, so that it made quite a good, irritating report on the top of the table. Smack! "George, how mean can you be?" No reply. He's away inside his head peering into some empty room, lonely and forsaken. Men are very delicate and neurotic these days, and curl up like wood-lice and go quite grey if you're sharp with them. I know now he's going to be nasty all the way upstairs and into bed. He'll put on his pyjamas in a depressed way, as if giving up the ghost, and then turn on his side without a word, and lie there suffering terribly and enjoying every moment of it. I can never make out whether he's got too many scruples in life, or none at all. Either way he always makes out a very good case for himself, since all his values are in order and invariable. I've started trying to make out my own case too, but I don't have that absolute belief which is necessary if you're to make converts. And that, after all, is the whole point of case-making.

So really it was the malevolent emanation from George's back lying there in its dark-blue printed silk pyjama-top that started off my gout.

It says here: "a disease of disordered metabolism." "Hereditary"; that means it's been lying around waiting for me, and only needed a few liquid lunches with Jenny and a sulky pyjama back to assert itself.

Oh my toe! I've got it propped up at the end of the bed, it's as red as a red-hot poker, and so sensitive that if Fritz opens the bedroom door to bring me a glass of milk (coffee is forbidden) I can feel the breeze and call out smartly: "Be careful! You're near the left side of my foot over there! Don't go down near the foot of the bed, because you could jolt it. Just hand me the glass, and keep clear. Don't circle round like that, please Fritz. Every time you circle my foot registers it with a new wave of lava. Listen—can you make me up a bowl of hot water and bicarbonate of soda? It's time to bathe it again. You know what the doctor said? 'We have to control the level of your uric acid, my dear, like the level of the water in a swimming pool.' I didn't even know I had uric acid! Now he calls it '*my* uric acid'! And I don't like that bit about the swimming pool either. Doctors are far too scientific these days. I don't want a scientist. I want someone to tell me I'm fabulous. (No, not *you*, Fritz.) Directly they do that, I jump up as fit as a fiddle. Ow! It's raging!"

I have a definite feeling, once I've said all this, that nobody loves me, except possibly Claudi. Billy merely appreciates me and to be appreciated you have to be amusing, well-dressed, well-informed and calm. The Bloater loves himself and the bed towards which he's hurrying, unwashed.

I go back to Th*e Cheerful Home Doctor.* Thank heavens this book is out of date. It's full of herbal remedies and superstitions. Also, another surprise; if you're ill, it actually recommends that you go to bed until you're better! No instant pills, no twenty-four-hour cures which send you staggering on to the streets with dilated eyes, greeting your friends and pretending to be normal because all your symptoms have been taken away and you can't produce a reason for the death-agony you feel.

Going over the detailed literature and hair-raising drawings, I feel I have everything. What's this? "Gouty deposits in the rims of the ears." I quickly go over the rims of my ears; how prehistoric they are. They've been living up there on my head for years, and this is the first time I've explored them with anything like interest. I remember an experienced man who once kissed me, thoughtfully covering up my ears with his hands, so as to shut me off from the outside world and engross me still more in his kiss. Whereas I prefer to be wide-awake and totally engrossed at the same time, since living at the top of your ability, unified and in touch with everything, is the prerequisite of successful physical contact. There are people going about who lick your ears too, if you give them half a chance. I imagine the right ear-licker would be fine; but the wrong one … the wrong one would bring up a gouty deposit on the spot.

I seem to be all right at the moment. "A gouty hand is shown in Fig. 13." Oh gruesome! All knobs like the top of my grandmother's cane. And it takes up three-quarters of a page, almost as much as the diagram showing a rheumatic heart. I stare at it glumly, meditating.

Claudi's cat, which lives two doors away, has come in and is looking at me with the same sort of stare I've been giving the gouty hand; unblinking distaste. This cat is called Plim-Plam and looks like a small lion; it has absolute confidence in the world, like the Queen reviewing her troops. It goes round the bottom of the bed like a seaside wave, and reappears well away, pressed up under the window. After another uninhibited scrutiny (can this be like Jenny's guitarist?) it rises up and places itself on the window-sill where it proceeds to look disinterestedly out of the window. Full marks, Plim!

Why do I always feel like a courtesan when I'm lying in bed and Plim walks round the room? I'm suddenly aware of my underwear laid over the back of the chair, when outside it's broad daylight and August into the bargain. Yes, Plim is like the Bloater, it makes a bedroom much more bedroomy. I suppose the fact that it's so at ease and so dignified, picking its way over blankets which have fallen off the bed and dragged with them a rubble of books, letters, remedies, mirrors, and pamphlets on cosmetics, I suppose all this suggests that I normally receive courtly animals and people in such circumstances. But isn't it too much like sickroom at school, and my groaning—isn't that more like a schoolboy's death-rattle than the magnificent paroxysm of *une grande horizontale*?

At least the doctor has told me that gout is a "young disease" these days. "Haven't you noticed those young execu-
tives, the twenty-six-year-old sheiks hobbling with a stick?
There are dozens of them about in the streets, entirely due
to our high standard of living."

Fritz brings me a blue plastic washing-up bowl with hot
water lurching to and fro in it. He says Claudi is at the
front door, and is asking for his cat. Oh, so that's it! People
always think you are trying to entice away their animals
with love and food, and they suspiciously follow up likely
trails and then confront you with the bare-faced theft of a
beloved creature. Whereas the brute facts are very different; strange dogs and cats are perpetually trying to force
their way into the house, and, if possible, sneak upstairs
and inhabit a bedroom. You find them strolling in at the
front door, possessing the rugs and twisting their heads
around for new excitements like journalists. On the whole,
and again like journalists, *any* future is to them preferable
to their present life, from which they are always escaping.
Plim is here because it finds you unbearable, Claudi! I,
with my gout and my blue bowl of hot water, represent
the new, the mysterious and unattainable. And tomorrow,
as a young sheik hobbling with a stick, my allure will be
doubled.

But in the meantime I decide to stick it out as a *grande
horizontale* and ask Fritz to bring Claudi up to talk to me.
Claudi loathes people who are ill; he himself has never had
a day's illness in his life, although he once vomited after
a caviar sandwich. I can hear him coming upstairs slowly
and reluctantly. A minute later he presents himself in the
doorway and peers into the room as though into a coffin.

"Come in, Claudi." My voice is succulent.

"Are you ill, my dear?"

"Yes, darling. I've got gout, one of the great horizontal diseases."

"Oh, then you must give up sweetbreads." (He's found a chair close to the door; sits down on it and looks at his watch; life presses.)

"What a silly thing to say. Am I the sort of person who eats sweetbreads in the first place?"

"I don't know your habits, my dear. I would not presume."

He's caught sight of the bowl of hot water (another invalid horror) and is already planning his escape. Still, he's got to buy his way to the door with some cheering-up talk. He goes on about the sweetbreads (I can distinctly feel the level of uric acid rising in my swimming pool):

"When you think of the terrible poverty and starvation in India, my God, you feel so helpless. And the things we throw away here. The other day I had to throw away a half a loaf of bread and I felt dreadful. You know what the Finance Minister of Pakistan said to me: 'If only I had your dustbins ...' And think of what they throw away in America!"

He certainly is rubbing it in about the sweetbreads. I fight back: "But, darling, there's never anything in your dustbin. You live off the smell of an oil-rag, you know you do. It's no good the Finance Minister of Pakistan getting excited about your dustbin, it's full of chickweed from your garden. A cheque from your bank account would be far more to the point."

The arrow finds its mark and Claudi decides this is the correct social moment to recognise his cat sitting on the window-sill. He gives an exclamation:

"Plim! What are you doing here?"

"It forced its way in. And it's moulting all over the carpet."

Claudi makes a forward plunge to lay hands on his cat.

"Look out!"

"What is it? What is it?" He reels back, bewildered.

"My toe! You took it by surprise with that sudden movement. Do be careful. Oh, Claudi, you've made it all angry and raging again, too bad of you."

"But I'm nowhere *near* your foot, sweetie-pie."

"Yes, but you're making wild involuntary movements suddenly. And you could easily reach it from there, unless I restrained you."

"Now Min, Min, Min. You are really a naughty little girl, lying in bed giving orders all the time to a poor elderly gentleman who comes to call on you, with love in his heart."

"Who only just comes to call on me, by accident, because he's looking for his pussycat . . . Yea," I put on some psalmlike unction, "when I was sick ye very nearly visited me not."

Claudi laughs slightly, but he still has the nagging feeling that he's missing life. He now sees a legitimate means of escape, and takes it.

"Well, Min, I can see that you are well on the way to recovery. And my presence is not really needed here any longer—"

I groan, and fold my arms across my chest like a corpse.

"Now, come on, what is it?" His heart smites him, but with the minimum of force.

"How would you like to have your big toe swollen up in this ridiculous way? And I very much doubt whether it will ever go down again. The least you could do is to look at it."

"Well, if I must."

He looks at it doubtfully; then he tries to take some sort of interest in it. He makes a statement in his legal voice:

"The main thing is that the two toes should be identical in size."

This is so ridiculous that we both start laughing. I sing out:

"All right! All right! Go away. You've done your bit. Go

out into the sunshine and drink the fresh air, and leave me here, ageing rapidly in a back bedroom." (I wonder why Claudi always makes me carry on like this?)

At the words "ageing rapidly" he really gets agitated.

"You say that to me, an old man nearly seventy and on the threshold of Heaven knows what!"

We're silent. Each goes back into himself, and takes up the position of Rodin's Thinker. There's a long, fruitful lull, broken by Plim-Plam jumping on heavy paws down from the window, which now bores it stiff. The same flowing sauntering promenade round the bed, intercepted by Claudi who gathers it up in his arms in a rock-the-baby position which shows all the curled white fur on its belly, like fine infant's petticoats.

Suddenly a thought strikes me, and I sit bolt upright in bed and wail:

"Claudi, it's tomorrow morning the Bloater's coming!"

"Well, my dear, I'm sure you can cope with him. You cope with me very well."

"Yes, but you're not trying to seduce me."

"How do you know, my dear?" Claudi has become very still and is looking at me intently. I have a feeling he may sit down on the edge of the bed—near my toe! I snap out:

"You're in love with your garden."

"No, my dear. I am not." Still horribly intent (I get a flash of insight into the difficulties of courtesan life).

"Claudi, if you don't help me I'll—"

"All right, my little Min. I'm just teasing you for a moment." He wasn't. "What time is he coming?"

"He's invited himself to coffee at eleven." I'm in a blue funk now. "And here I am lying helpless in bed. In *bed*. And that rissole, that bedsore, that Judas Iscariot will—"

Claudi gives me a strange disbelieving glance full of

analytic scepticism. The trouble with men who know everything about women is that they don't believe a word you say, and this is catching. In the end you don't believe yourself either. Just listen to Claudi:

"Well now, to begin with I don't think you should have on any black lace underwear. Just wear those Viyella pyjamas, sweetie-pie, they would put anyone off."

"Do they put you off?"

"Not—too much. But then I can't expect the very best at my age."

"There is nothing more sexy than a good, *clean* pair of pale yellow Viyella pyjamas."

"Well then, I advise you to stick to the black lace."

"*How am I to get him out of the house?*"

"All right. We'll make a little plan. Now ... suppose he stays for one hour. Or are you going to give the poor man one hour and a half?"

"Oh God, please stop being on his side. I'm too ill for the sex-war."

"One hour and a half brings us to half past twelve. Well now, at half past twelve I'll come to the front door and ring the bell."

"No, it's too obvious. You'll start laughing."

"I'll ring the bell and come in, and I'll sit down and tell funny stories, and I won't go away."

"But we'll be there until four o'clock!"

He looks insulted, and I'm choking with mirth because of course I've told the truth! I make it up at once:

"Darling, it's a wonderful plan. But look, couldn't I keep you *in reserve* so to speak? I mean, there's always a chance he'll leave of his own accord."

"All right then. At half past twelve if he hasn't gone, you ring me up on the telephone."

"What shall I say?"

"You can just order some greengroceries or something."

"I think I'd better order some fish. I never have my greengroceries delivered."

"Yes, well then you order some fish, and I come round in a striped apron and hit him over the head with a fish-monger's cudgel."

"You promise you won't laugh?"

"Sweetie-pie, I promise!"

Back to The *Cheerful Home Doctor* for another hour before tea. I stew my toe, and will it to go down. I read the newspapers and get a vague impression that somebody is running the country, but who is it exactly? I rearrange all the facts of my life to slightly better advantage. I repeat the opening lines of a little ditty that Jenny and I made up after our deep-confidence lunch: "I was feeling simply awful (pronounced 'offal') when I went into that brothel ..." Are we fully adult, responsible pillars of society? Certainly; it's simply that we're allowed two or three safety valves nowadays, and rank silliness is one of them. You cannot listen to electronic sound for seven hours a day, and keep sane without it.

Ah, here comes Racquel, my dangerous woman friend! She and she alone knows how to manage her life; she seems to be above love affairs, always fully occupied with a teeming diary of quite boring appointments—everything seems to have equal value. I could never imagine her being shaken because a man lay across her foot; hmm ... I'm putting her in this hypothetical situation and trying her out. Here's her foot and here's his stomach. Contact; Racquel remains perfectly still, but instead of ticking him off as I thought she would, she's—leaning over very boldly and sliding her fingers into the dark hair! Inside my head of course! Oh well, who knows?

She's brought her sewing (she never wastes a minute) and is fresh, plump and cheerful. I hate sewing (which is almost as boring as looking at beautiful views) but I take up the hem of a skirt a little too far so as to make it ultra-ultra-fashionable. I get along fast with big stitches, while Racquel (an architect) talks that reassuring normal talk which seemed to go out with one's grandparents.

"Min, why do you sew from left to right?"

"I didn't know I did. Anyway it doesn't matter which way you sew. If you turn the material round you're going in the opposite direction. And I get there just the same."

"I know. But it's like trying to read the Koran and beginning in the top left-hand corner."

I'm puzzled by this left to right business, and my brain fogs up as if I'm trying to change lire into francs. I know that Racquel knows the correct way of doing everything, and I haven't a hope. So I fall back on inconsequential eleven-year-old chatter:

"Not content with all this sewing now, do you know I even dreamt I was sewing the other night? I was sewing a sampler for an elephant who was dictating the motto to me. This motto was to be embroidered in big, red capital letters, and the elephant was to wear it across its chest. And do you know what the motto was?"

Racquel gives me the sort of look people give to the compulsive dream-teller:

"No. What?"

"'Advance or retreat, it's all the same to me.'"

I'm afraid I collapse and laugh heartily; after all, it's my dream, and I naturally find it hilarious. Racquel has courteously put her head on one side, and is looking puzzled.

Bother; she certainly has some blind spots, this worldly-wise one.

"What had you been eating?"

I'm disgusted with her, and snap out:

"Fish fingers!" No, no, I must *not* be so irritable. I explain it all: "It's probably the result of watching those poor elephants at Regent's Park Zoo, Racquel. You know they can only step backwards or forwards."

"What would be the Freudian interpretation?"

"Give me three days and a sofa." Yes, it must be the gout which is making me so snappy. I try again humbly: "I think it means that I'm impeded in the main course of my life, and that the Bloater is making me embroider samplers which he'll hang on his chest after the conquest. He's stepping backwards and forwards, taking all the applause and attention, before trumpeting out his masculine aria: 'Ummm-m-m!'"

Racquel bites off her piece of cotton and says:

"You're better."

4

He's here. Oh! He's rather special. He arrived at ten-thirty, and was delighted when I opened the front door to him in a dressing-gown. He's brought me a present; a first edition of one of D'Annunzio's plays, you tie it with green velvet ribbons. I'm a bit wary. Does this make me the Duse?

There's no question that I'm pleased with this present; I love books that you can lock up with a fastening like a suitcase, or tie up like a nightgown. Also, he's slower than usual about sitting down, usually he goes down like a meal-sack into the first chair. But this time he stands about in the sitting-room and inclines himself over me at a worshipping but restrained angle. This brings out the best in me, and I start being very charming. I do a number of unnecessarily delicate and amusing things, which used to make my grandmother call me her "lily-white angel."

His shirt seems to fill up the great divide between the lapels of his suit, like rumpled white paper—as though some composer just wrote a line on it and then scrunched it up. His tie today is magenta with red spots (aren't we getting warmer as regards the elephant's sampler?), and the handkerchief, matching again, is really lolling out like a thirsty tongue.

Even more extraordinary, no smell. Not a whiff. I don't like it. He's taken abnormal precautions, obviously out for a quick kill. And why doesn't he start boring me? What's happened? Surely I can't be as sex-starved as all that? No; it's just that he's keeping silent for fear of irritating me with his rich, vibrating voice. How wise of him! Oh dear. He's much cleverer than I thought.

What a lot of hair the Bloater has! Curious; I never bothered to look at his head before, but now I see that there's masses and masses of thick dark hair, some seems to be curly and there are streaks of very shiny grey. Not at all bad, and quite a temptation for a head-hunter. But I'm not a head-hunter. I just want to be left alone to get on with my gout. I've been talking about him far too much in the last few days and I've built him up into something. Whereas he's just a stupid old jumbo-sized baritone.

You know what he's waiting for, don't you? The first course; that's when he makes me behave so badly that I have to apologise to him. I flick my mouth into a whiplash smile. He seems dazed by this.

Hullo. I think he's going to sink down now. He's getting very near that piano stool. His legs are wilting. Ah, he's down. He certainly knows how to occupy a piano stool and have a real rest on it.

I *refuse* to make conversation; it's tiring, and I'm an invalid. Of course we already know each other very well indeed, and hardly have to talk. I maintain my deathly silence right to the end; and finally he says casually:

"I like your dressing-gown."

This instantly annoys me. I redouble the quality of my silence. Trying to lead off with a bedroom remark is not the way to get into my good graces. I freeze him and freeze him. Just when I think I've won, he says with the same casualness—and exactly as though we've been having a conversation:

"You know, I can't get through to most women. But I feel a great *rapport* with you."

The impudence of it. And there's a gloss on his eyeballs like fine Chinese porcelain. I believe he had Sicilian grandparents.

"Really!" (You should hear my dry, ferret's cough!) "Then it's a very one-sided *rapport*."

After a pause, he laughs with real pleasure. Oh what a pest! He's already started dining off my nerves.

"That may be the reason." He looks away as though it's too important to live with. "I mean your honesty may be the reason."

"Honesty! How dare you say that? Cheating and double-dealing are my speciality. And don't think I'm going to give you the pleasure of either."

I'm passing him at this moment, and he suddenly touches my arm with a restraining gesture which makes me jump back as if he's got scabies. He says gently: "I didn't mean to annoy you."

"You didn't annoy me." (Huh!) "I'm probably a bit sharp and irritable with this foot trouble, and I'm afraid it makes me rather bad company."

Apologising already; don't say the Bloater isn't crafty. I'm furious with myself. I add:

"And I don't mind if I am bad company."

Another pause, and another laugh of the same kind. Ha-ha-ha. We're getting back to normal after all; although there were two or three minutes when he kept his sensibility well back in its kennel and I was quite definitely attracted. I've forgotten all about the first-edition D'Annunzio with green ribbons now, and I ask acidly:

"By the way are you less blocked than you used to be?"

The Bloater went to a psychiatrist when he was singing in Rome last year, and ever since then he's spoken of being "blocked." I think this means he's less good at seducing women than formerly. He once told me he'd slept with fifty or sixty, so the "blocking" is something relatively new. He treats my question with serious interest, as though I'd asked with concern in my voice, and says:

"It's getting a bit better, thank you. I think if I had more commerce with people, it would help. For example, if I had more normal dealings with people, I'd know how to talk to you."

"Don't you know how to talk to me?" (Careful!)

"No. I never know what to say next." This is accompanied by a very dark honest glance, and a shake of the head. (That's right; put yourself at my mercy and let me trample all over you. For a man who doesn't have commerce with people, your skill is abnormal.) I pass it off lightly:

"Everyone has that trouble. Just make it up as you go along."

He ponders this, as if it were a real contribution. Then unselfishly (!) tries to put the best complexion on his trouble with this priceless remark:

"Oh, don't worry. I think I'm gradually unblocking. And you know," a sly look at me, "you're a great help."

You—animal! With your blocking and unblocking. Do you imagine for one moment that I want to be a help? I do not! You can unblock yourself all alone. How can you be so absurd, taking yourself so seriously and talking the sort of nonsense neurotic women talk? If you knew how less masculine it made you, you'd drop it on the spot.

"… Although sometimes," he hasn't finished yet, "you make me feel I'm dull."

It's my moment, and I take it with a burst of laughter:

"I'm very glad to hear it."

Now you must admit that was vicious. No one has an ox-hide which can keep out a remark like that. I must have done horrible damage inside. He seems to be making a little choking noise. Oh God, I *have* smashed him. How terrible. A great big man like that too, it seems to make it far worse. I go up impulsively and touch his head and press a kiss on his brow, noting as I do so that it's fine, smooth and slightly moist.

"Sorry."

His arms close around me, and I'm still looking down on the top of the head, conscience-struck, when it's pushed back and the Bloater's face appears and says with a superior smile:

"I always find what you say interesting."

Not a ripple on the surface. He hasn't even felt it!

"Let me go!" I'm wild, and have already made a pair of fists.

"Why?" says the idiotic face.

"Because I'm ill and in pain."

There's a slight loosening in the grip; the face presses itself against my dressing-gown and says with humorous, muffled lust:

"Well, I'll make you better."

"Carlos, will you please let me go. My foot hurts."

He unbinds his arms, and turns away as if I've insulted him. I hobble out of reach, sit down and prop my foot up. If it was anyone else, I'd talk to cover up the situation, but I simply know him too well, and don't bother. Besides, it's not necessary; a moment later he's drumming on the piano with his fingers. And look—smiling at me! I feel very worn and defeated. Isn't it time to phone Claudi?

I say feebly, hardly convincing myself:

"I really ought to phone up the fishmonger's."

"Let me get something for you."

"No, no," I make peevish invalid's movements, "it's not necessary. They bring it to the door."

"Well, you tell me what you want, and I'll do the telephoning for you." He stands up, and is all alacrity and consideration.

"No, I'd much rather you tried the piano. I've just had it tuned, and I know your ear is ultra-perfect. Would you do that for me, Carlos?"

Can he resist an appeal to his vanity? He cannot. Even the fact that what I've asked him to do is beneath him doesn't register. He slews his head round and looks at the piano.

"Is that it?" Why do people ask questions like that, I wonder. I reply:

"Certainly not. I keep it in the kitchen built into the sink unit."

"I see." His response is definitely firmer this time; there may yet be hope for us. He sits down again, plucks open the lid, and bends with a lifetime of longing over the keyboard as if it was the body of a woman. (No. 61.) Then, with infinite strength and delicacy, he starts on it. Oh! Oh! Oh! that's better. He has absolute authority, and regains every shred of personality he's lost in the last half-hour. So long as he doesn't sing, the emotional barometer may go up again. I enjoy seeing him press on the pedals, the clutch and the accelerator. With that handkerchief dripping blood out of his pocket, and the dip of his concentrating head, he's on the verge of being fabulous. MacFisheries can wait a bit.

The hard core of the trouble with the Bloater is that most of the time he's not real *to me*. To someone else he may personify reality. I think he must have booked into too many not quite first-class hotels and this has simply become his milieu. And then he must have climbed on to too many platforms; and men get this infection, this "platformitis," much more easily than women. The men who are absolutely like oneself are the dangerous ones. Do I mean Billy?

At this moment the telephone rings, and I tremble in case the fishmonger has taken the initiative and is phoning me. It's Jenny. She's having one of her tea-breaks at the sound workshop. She's in the wars, just like me. She's been burnt, right at the top of her thigh! I at once think of the guitarist:

"What happened?"

"I was sitting in a coffee bar with a very fascinating middle-aged man who said he was psychic. Well, there was a mechanic from the local garage who came and sat down on the other side of me. Then there was a curious sort of silence, because we both stopped talking, and I had the feeling that my psychic man was somehow trying to bend the will of the other boy to make him go away."

"Oh dear." (The Bloater plays "tum-te-tum.")

"Instead of going away, the boy suddenly overturned his hot coffee—on to me! And I was wearing tightfitting chenille trousers, so the boiling coffee soaked right in, it was agony."

"What did you do? Scream out like a scalded cat?"

"No, I went on sitting there without moving a muscle, because I was somehow being spiritually conned by my psychic man."

"Don't be silly." This isn't at all like Jenny.

"Well, I just felt I mustn't make a scene in public. It suddenly became terribly important. Then my psychic took me off to hospital in a taxi to get it dressed."

"Who is this psychic? Is he new on the scene?"

"In a way. He's my insurance against the guitar."

"Meaning to say that if you're covered with burns you can't make love to your guitar?"

"No. He's supposed to bolster up my ego, so that what-ever the guitar does I shan't care."

"And what has the guitar been doing?" There are more polite noises off from the Bloater, so I know he's begun to listen in. He plays very lightly.

"He's a monster!" Jenny howls down the telephone.

"I knew it."

"He asked me to lunch. And I said: 'All right, where?' And he said: 'Oh, I hate meals out, they're so bad. I'd like to cook something special for you.'"

"Oh boy, you didn't fall for that one!"

"Well, honestly it's very difficult not to look ridiculous. I just said I didn't like being in enclosed spaces. And he said: 'We'll have the windows open.'"

"You could say he has a sort of lousy honesty. At least he didn't say: 'All right, we'll lunch out, just look in at my place for a drink on the way,' and when you get there you find him making meat balls and rice, or any other terrible slop which he thinks is the price of some ghastly sort of advance he's going to make."

We agree heartily on this. There is dead silence from the sitting-room.

Jenny says morosely:

"I gave him strict instructions. I said I must have pota-toes, I must have *food*. I thought it would keep him busy. And when I arrived, not a potato in sight."

"He probably thought you were incredibly smooth, and this was all a blind."

"Just tinned salmon, mashed up in a wooden bowl to look interesting, and some lettuce leaves."

"Worse than our fifth-rate cheddar cheese and barley wine."

"I ate up every single morsel, really hating him."

"Oh good!"

"But then I felt sleepy."

"Jenny!"

"Honestly, I couldn't help it. I was dead tired when I arrived."

"So I suppose you lay down, being a child of nature." I'm a bit snappy to her.

"I did lie down, Min. And so did he. And we just rested, side by side, like two little goody-goodies."

I groan; I know what's coming next. I say:

"And then I suppose he kissed you on your brow, just at the phony old hairline?" The phone is silent, recording my direct hit. "They always do. And you told me he had a sense of timing. You said he *knew everything*."

"Listen: I spent three days *longing* for his mouth! It's lethal, lethal! And Min, he shudders every few seconds when he's touching me, with a really violent controlled shudder. I've just never felt anything like it. And his lips are round, not flat—and do you know, that makes all the difference."

My finger instinctively moves up to my mouth; round or flat? Nothing much there at all. Just something pouting, and then you're in to the teeth. I say wearily:

"Then I suppose you went to bed with him?"

"No. I remembered the potatoes. And I stopped."

"Because he didn't give you any potatoes!" I'm really delighted with her. "What an excellent reason!"

"Yes, but I've seen his chest. And I want him dreadfully."

"Pooh! What's a chest?"

"This one's absolutely smooth, with thick rounded shoulders. And it shudders when it's near me."

I reflect that you really can't ask much more than that. So I say disgustedly:

"This is all very objective, Jenny. But what sort of *person* is he, for God's sake?"

"Quick as a flash, very pop Cambridge, I told you, success and plastic high living. He'd flit through any kind of situation without turning a hair."

"He sounds genuinely nasty."

"He almost is. But, you know, when you begin to make love to someone, if they're nasty inside you can't go on. Well, he's unselfish in making love."

"This is serious."

"I know."

I leave the telephone rather shaken. For the moment I've totally forgotten the Bloater, it's like the night when I switched out the light in the kitchen while George was eating his evening meal, locked the door behind me, and went thoughtfully upstairs to bed. It took me three months to live that down.

I re-enter the sitting-room, forgetting to hobble because my mind's not on it, and start reading an old letter which is lying on the table: "I don't like Spain as much as I did, although I have seen a lot while I've been in Barcelona ..."

Someone moves in the room, and I give a start.

"Oh, Carlos. How are you?" I'm distracted, but he's full of glowing lechery and says:

"I'm afraid I couldn't help hearing part of your conversation."

What a ham-fisted opening! How could he? Where is the palm-court orchestra? Where are Vicki Baum and *Grand Hotel*?

"I kept my voice as low as possible. It was a personal matter." Sorry, I forgot, the Bloater never squirms. He just enters into things with a wholeheartedness that is nauseating. So he says:

"I knew that. Is she—in some sort of trouble?"

"She doesn't know whether to go to bed with a man, because he attracts her too much and doesn't give her any potatoes."

"Oh-ha. It's quite a normal situation then."

I'm slightly interested in his response and ask:

"What makes you say that?"

"The abnormal situation is—when the woman doesn't know that she's attracted by the man."

There is a deafening silence. I daren't move in case I cause an explosion. I'm riveted against the table, staring at "although I have seen a lot while I've been in Barcelona ..."

Oh, you clever old Bloater! I suddenly get a flashback to a night in a restaurant when he listed his passions: "Women, my own voice, my own body, money, lobster." How could I underestimate a declaration as naïve, as experienced as that? But the word lobster saves me; fish, of course, what I need is a fish.

I go to the telephone without a word and dial Claudi's number.

Claudi replies so quickly that I'm put off, and say doubtfully:

"Hullo. Is that MacFisheries?"

"Yes, madam," says Claudi firmly in his character actor's voice.

"Oh well—" I'm dumbfounded for a moment by the way he's caught the spirit of the thing, and then a convulsive, agonizing mirth shakes my whole body. I gasp out: "Well, could you send round a ..." Here I pause and rack my brains for the name of a single fish; the Atlantic, the Pacific are full of them, and the only thing I can think of is lobster. Surely that won't do. Isn't it just the thing to increase the uric acid in my swimming pool? Yes, gout and lobster obviously go together. Think of something, quickly! What's the next thing to a lobster? A prawn. And how do they sell prawns? By the—the what? Quickly! "Could you send round a measure of prawns?"

That's done it. An experienced fishmonger would snap

out some tart reply; I realise there's no such thing as a "measure" of prawns. It didn't feel right when I said it. Claudi answers warmly:

"Yes, madam. Certainly madam. Will that be all?"

By now I'm racked and in pain, with the laughter leaking out of my nose and my ears. If only he wasn't so deadly serious! I'm helpless, weak as a sapling U-shaped by a gale-force wind. Make an effort! Finally I get out in a gagged voice:

"Yes, thank you. Can you let me have it in about an hour?"

"*In about an hour?*" asks Claudi, thunderstruck.

There's a dead silence between us. Oh God, Claudi's taken it literally. We're at cross purposes, and if I don't say something quickly he'll wait an hour before coming in. This is what comes of over-playing the part you're given; he's ruining everything. I must now be very convincing and yet casual.

"Or as soon as you can." I do that quite well; Claudi catches on at once and we're saved again.

"I'll be right round, madam," he says sternly, and rings off.

It's only when I put down the phone that I remember I haven't given my name or address. I hobble upstairs on my gouty foot and stuff a handful of clothing in my mouth and lie on my bed making spasms like a spastic.

5

I'm having dinner with Billy tonight. George is working late, but he may join us afterwards. He's got over the sulking fit and has had a good time organising my gout. (George is very good at the preservation and day in, day out maintenance of the human body.) Consequently it's better; you only have to take an interest in something, and it responds. Under the influence of The *Cheerful Home Doctor* I've become very much aware of natural phenomena: herbs and rainy weather, for example. I can sum up people's nutritional deficiencies from the patchy look on their faces, or the way they sit. Poisonous berries are *everywhere*. Then there are my own superstitions. I've got this unlucky green ring which may have been the influential subliminal starter of the whole gout syndrome. I've just buried it in the front garden, and of course Claudi caught me and asked me if I was weeding. We don't speak much since our disgraceful behaviour the other day; it worked like a charm I may say, but it's a low, disreputable way for two grown-up people to behave (and one of them a man of sixty). When we don't speak, we look at each other and tears come into our eyes. I've stuck a little wafer of wood into the ground over my ring, and on the orange label with the washed-out name of some rose on it, I've written: "my ring." Claudi says that will be the first thing a burglar will do; he'll come up and read the label and dig for treasure—and lo and behold I'll never have gout again! Claudi always spanks me on the behind when we're in the garden. He does it rather badly, and mutters under his breath: "Go away with you, Min."

Tonight my bedroom is all set for the *grande toilette*. I always dress up for Billy because he's so elegant. On my unmade bed are pots and pots of make-up, none of which I shall use. This eye make-up, for example, every time I put it on people tell me I look ill. And I'm supposed to pluck my eyebrows to make them the right shape, and then I meet Racquel who has very fair gingery eyebrows and she cries: "Don't! If you only knew what it was like not to have any eyebrows. I have to draw mine on." "But, Racquel, what on earth will you do when you wake up beside the man you love one morning with no eyebrows?" She gives me the same mysterious look whenever I mention men; with her freshly ironed blouses fitting so well over her bosom, she looks choice but untouched. Possibly she's frigid. But don't those blouses fit a little too well?

That settles the eye question. I'll just mix up some mascara and have done with it. I dip my narrow wooden mascara brush (very Nefertiti) into the whisky and soda which I've poured myself, and hope my eyelashes don't drop off half-way through the evening. What a long, boring business this dressing-up is. I switch on the Third Programme and as usual it's a working-class play. I give it the sort of avid attention one gives to the same programme which has been running for five years.

I must say this silver-kid dress is rather nice, it's the co-lour of a saxophone and would drive the Bloater mad! I get the feeling that if I ever get closer to the Bloater he will literally half-kill me. Why, why, why, does he put up with me? And why don't I desire him, so big and tempting and reassuring? Billy's only half a head taller than myself, but he has only to snap his fingers and it means something. He's so gay, so serious. Very occasionally if we've got a little drunk at dinner he takes my hand and holds it, giving it a gentle flowing pressure, indescribably pleasing and nourishing—and almost impossible to break off.

Shall I wear bare legs and these almost non-existent sandals with slightly vulgar diamantés on them? Yes, with the covering fire of Billy's most proper dark suit they'll look rainy and perfect. Although walking on my own in the street they'd be so flashy I'd have to take them off and go barefoot.

Damn. This lip gloss is nearly finished; that means going all the way to Woolworth's. And I'm working tomorrow.

Another thing about Billy: in his attitude to sex he's an aristocrat, he understands it and adores it. And he lets me run down other men by the hour. Also, he's quite capable of loving someone and keeping it up for years. Or has he been a bachelor too long for that? To sum up: I'm completely at ease with him. Just as I'm on edge with the B., nagged and torn and jangled. I've got the feeling that one of these two men is a very good lover, but which one? You just can't tell from the outside, all the relevant information is hermetically sealed away in their senses, in their imaginations, in their courage, and in their response to me. What would London be like without its superlative middle-aged men? Empty and desolate.

Powder. I give myself a really good look in the mirror. Ow! I can hear Racquel again: "I always powder against the grain." What does that mean? Upwards. I powder upwards. How knowledgeable other women are; what deep lives they have. I always get as much powder on my nose as I possibly can, and that's it. (Liar.) Now Jenny is too busy going from situation to situation to tackle anything like a complete face. She says: "I don't think you should look into someone's face too deeply. Just take the whole thing as a going concern."

Yes, it's true. I'm really glowing like Lucifer tonight, this black strapless bra actually fits me and is tartiness personified; I've a good mind to go out like this and crush London underfoot. I go on gilding myself for another three-quarters of an hour, really boiling with daring. Is there anything I can't do? Just let me pass the wet scent-stopper up the inside of my arm … annoying, I'm getting flushed with victory and it always coarsens my skin. I try to think cold, calm thoughts, and do it easily. Good heavens, how worldly I am! I'm so well finished, I feel as though I've been dipped in some sort of classical French *ennui* and crisped before serving.

"Billy! You're handsome, you're handsome, I swear it!"

"You look pretty, Min."

"What luck. I've been slaving away for an hour, scraping things on and off. And you know, Billy, being unhappy is very bad for your features, they won't sit properly on your face. When George snapped at me last week, my nose simply went out of control."

"I thought it was your foot."

"You're not to make me laugh before ten-thirty!"

"Why, what happens then?"

"We've eaten, and you're feeling fond of me, and if I give a dreadful cackling laugh it won't matter."

"Oh yes it will! I shall notice it on the spot. Besides, I'm fond of you now."

Billy is far too sensible to follow that with any sort of caress. He knows I would only snap out: "Don't touch me!" at this stage; people who say ten-thirty mean ten-thirty.

In the restaurant we haven't been sitting there for a moment before the table becomes Billy's table, and even the corner of the room seems to be better than the other corners, darker, redder, perhaps I mean wealthier. Although Billy isn't very well off. Oh, I've just remembered; he was married years ago, and had a divorce. Basically this makes him less attractive, because the scars always make people harder. Perhaps I can get hard enough to cope with it. That thought about the corner of the restaurant reminds me of Claudi being funny about street-corners in alien parts of London: "My God is there anything more foreign, more depressing, than other people's street corners? But how interesting, how unboring is your own familiar street-corner, and the streets filled with all the proper things leading off it." I tell Billy, who says:

"Yes, it's true. You know what Claudi's secret is, don't you? He never misses a meal and he never makes an enemy."

"Oh Billy! That's almost—a condemnation."

"Not really. It's only you and I who have this respect for excess. Most people would be very impressed by Claudi's control."

I have a sudden close-up of Claudi with his MacFisheries face on, really wicked, repeating: "Yes, madam, no, madam, three bags full, madam."

"I don't think he's very controlled."

"That's because you are his weakness."

"Do I make him behave badly?"

"Terribly badly."

I'm pleased, and eat my Parma ham smiling at Billy. He is eating something in a small brown pot, and smiles back, but attends to his pot at the same time. Claudi isn't the only one then who never misses a meal. But still Billy's divorce and his careful habits don't seem to have anything to do with the person inside him. I mean, they are extras, not mirrors.

"Billy, have you got hidden away at the back of your mind a picture of a woman with nice, big thighs? If so, I want to know *now*."

Billy thinks for a few seconds, then he looks over my head and makes his eyes slitty. At last he says truthfully:

"I don't—think so."

I'm very impressed.

"Do you always tell me the truth?" He's shocked and answers:

"Oh no. Certainly not. You've got to cheat a bit to make life work, you know."

"But people are always telling me to be chronological and to face facts."

"That's very bad. It's hopeless. Facing facts makes people very ill, sometimes it kills them."

"But what about the truth?"

"You tell the truth very often, as often as possible because it's such a pleasure. But you also tell lies of course. So you give good value."

"That's specious."

"Well, it is a bit! What I really loathe are people who say: 'I'm tactless and outspoken.' I always get up and move away when someone says that to me, they're quite likely to tell me something about myself I don't want to know."

"What I loathe are mean men who take women out and don't feed them. The girl I work with in the studio has one of those. They're usually fattish, and don't eat much themselves."

"Well, I'm fattish, and I eat masses." Billy is charming tonight.

"You're beautiful and highly desirable."

"You're supposed to tell a man he's handsome."

"You make me feel safe."

"Oh dear. I don't want to do that."

The laughter is running like a river under everything we say; now Billy has got his hands in his lap looking somehow as though they've been rejected and have slithered down there from my shoulders. I say:

"I mean, your values are stable. And it gives me back my childhood."

"Min, what touching things you say." He gets gentle.

"And I told you you were handsome when you first arrived. So you're getting greedy. Don't you need a spatula to get to the bottom of that pot?"

"I think this spoon is a kind of spatula. Please try to finish those olives or I shall feel like one of your mean men who don't feed you."

"I haven't got any men. I only know about one."

"One could be enough. If it was the right one."

I decide to put him on the spot, half for serious reasons and half for fun. And with an almost nasty smile, I say:

"Yes, but it never is, is it?"

Billy gives me a kissing look, but the waiter pushes in and we have to stop. So I shall never know what he was going to say. I've often wondered what it would be like being embraced by Billy. I flirt with him automatically but it seems to increase the distance between us. Billy has obviously been thinking exactly the same thing about me, because he asks:

"You're not in love with the Blo—with Fafner, are you?"

"Billy! Don't *you* start that too! Are you mad? Are you insane?"

"You talk about him a lot, you know."

"Because I can't stand the sight of him! Billy, you are my basic friend, my basic man, so of course I tell you everything. Is it boring?"

"No. It's like my schooldays sprinkled with champagne."

"So we both get childhood ... how wet!"

Billy isn't displeased, and looking at his sole *bonne femme* blames the shortcomings of the English on it by talking to it like this:

"Yes, it is wet, but it's the English view of things. Neapolitans say: life begins tomorrow. Either way you don't have to live *now*."

"But I want to!" I cry out sharply, almost a yap.

Billy turns towards me; one sees that the eyes and the hair are dark amber and the flesh has a fresh, roasted look. He smells exquisite.

"So do I," he says, straight into my face.

Plim-Plam is sitting between Racquel and myself listening to Chaliapin on an old gramophone record. It's putting up with the noise because Claudi has gone out and there's nothing else to do. Racquel is marvelling at Chaliapin's pear-shaped head on the sleeve of the disc. I gloat over it with the same sense of horror and mystery. His voice is past its prime in this recording, but that only increases his stature—you imagine all the rest.

"Do you think he was a heart-breaker, Racquel?" This is a sly question because what I want to know is if *she* is a heart-breaker.

"Well, he's well set up ..."

"Yes, but the angle of his shoulders is all wrong. You couldn't nestle against a sloping shoulder like that, you'd slide off to Australia."

"That's nothing to do with it," says Racquel almost sternly. "If the whole body has force ..."

"And his hair boiling up round the back of his head like a soufflé. No, no, I couldn't!"

"He's not asking you!" She's still pert, and seems to have taken on the part of protecting men of genius from me. Why does she do this? I'm determined to get at her secret.

"Do you always have to be asked *first*, Racquel?"

She's filing her nails, and has a pile of blue-tinted sketch plans on the floor beside her. Can't you imagine the specifying she'll do over them? Oh, she's so balanced and prissy it makes my blood boil. She's the sort of woman who'd give you a floodlit bedroom and on purpose. But she's going to reply to my question because she's in the habit of answering questions: "Can you explain the function of that linear recess?" or "Do you always have to be asked *first*?"

"Sometimes you sense that it's up to you." What an answer! I'm staggered, and say:

"Do you, Racquel? I don't. I never sense anything."

"That's because you're always so busy being yourself. You must be more receptive."

I was right. She's a dark horse. She's probably the most receptive woman in London. I'd better be careful. In a blinding flash I have an idea: try her on the Bloater! Weren't they made for one another! He's well set up too, and I haven't a doubt that "the whole body has force." Of course I'm absolutely positive deep down that the B. will loathe her. He'll take one look at her ginger eyelashes and make off. He won't even give her two out of ten. I'm bursting with slippery things to say, and try one of them:

"Do you think we're all getting more and more immoral?" I say this in my abbey voice, to inspire trust.

Again she's going to answer! Really, I'm almost ashamed of her for not being more devious.

"Well, I think careless women have brought down the price of flesh in the last few years."

The hat-trick! Who would have believed it? "The price

of flesh"—what a phrase! No need to go to the bookshop any longer and finger a few Penguins to find out what the current morality is; just ask Racquel. People ought to write up their love-lives and bring them to her to be redesigned. I stick out my gouty toe, which got a bit worse after that dinner with Billy, and think interestedly about the price of flesh.

"But how do you keep the price *up*, Racquel?"

She looks complacent; obviously the price of her flesh is gilt-edged at the moment. Mine isn't: so I listen humbly.

"Instinct. Wisdom. You learn to be selective."

Suddenly she's letting me down with platitudes. I'm bored and talk about the cat.

"The poor Plim will never be selective. Although I did hear it yodelling under a car the other night, so there's still something going on inside all that fur. I gave it the haddock milk today, so it's drunk on fishy milk. It's curious to have a lion about the place which contains a little flirt with fishy breath."

The door-bell rings. It's six o'clock, too early for George. I go to it, and open up carelessly. In steps the Bloater. Damn, damn, damn, I'm not ready, I've got gout. How dare he call without notice! I'm furious with myself, him, and Racquel. My tongue sticks in my mouth and I just repeat:

"But I thought you were in—in Bayreuth."

6

If you could see the three of us in the sitting-room, each posing and waiting for a cue, you'd give up your evening at Covent Garden without a murmur. The B. is just butting a lampshade and comes to rest dead centre, smiling first at Racquel and then at myself. He's got on a great big sweaty Diaghilev travelling coat, lined—I swear to you—with *red fur*. Yes, the saturated umbrella is there as a third leg, and the despatch-case, and a sort of dressing-case of waxed leather with some very medical-looking bumps on the side of it.

Racquel is taking him all in; Chaliapin to the life. Is she going to ogle him? Not at all, she's become more restful and adult than before. She even pulls down her skirt so that it jumps up and covers her legs a little bit less than it did. I don't like it. I'm at a disadvantage, and that makes me talk and hobble about as though I'm pig-in-the-middle.

The B. gives the impression that he's still travelling. He says "Ah!" once or twice and then opens his dressing-case and takes out a thermos flask. I'm stunned, and make gestures of withering disdain.

"What's in that, Carlos?"

"Soup."

Racquel says in a murmur you could hear from the Crystal Palace:

"Oh, poor man."

At this there's a glint of fire from the B.'s teeth and eyes.

I can feel an angry twitch in my gouty toe. I say coldly:

"What's poor about him? He's just been on a grand spree, rampaging all over Europe."

Racquel cleverly holds her tongue, and looks at the carpet long enough to suggest I've been rude to her.

The B. naturally trades on all this, and when he's worn it threadbare with his glinting looks, he begins slowly and carefully to unscrew the top of his thermos. I say:

"Carlos! You're not going to stand there and drink dirty old soup in the middle of the sitting-room!"

He stops with the mug-top in one hand and the loaded thermos in the other, trying to look pitiful but merely succeeding in looking idiotic. Then he craftily blurts out (no successful man over thirty-five *ever* blurts anything out):

"Well, where shall I drink it then?"

Of course the woman in Racquel (under the brickwork and the pelmets) rises up instantaneously. She makes an involuntary welcoming movement as though inviting him to bed down on the floor beside her sketch plans, where she will warm and comfort and specify *ad nauseam*. She says:

"You must be *frozen* after such a long journey."

The B., who was just about to take off his impresario coat in order to get down properly to the soup-drinking, keeps it on. I snap:

"In that Siberian bear's outfit? Hardly. It's as warm as toast in there, isn't it, Carlos?"

With my "isn't it, Carlos?" I'm just daring him to put me in the wrong. He dithers for a minute between the two of us, and then settles for an expressive "We-eell!" (He's still holding that inexpressibly vile thermos flask.)

"It's August." I remind him by the firmness of my voice and glance that if he goes an inch further there will be thunder and lightning.

"It isn't, actually," says Racquel, laughing, "it's the first of September today."

I contemplate her. How did she get in in the first place? I don't know the sort of people who know the date. The only people I get on with these days are those who are exhausted all the time, like myself. At the thought of my exhaustion, I feel twice as exhausted as I did a moment ago. I sink down with a moan, and play the introverted little pest. All right, Racquel, you win! I've suddenly realised what it is that's wrong with you: you have no neuroses, no problems.

Racquel says kindly to me:

"Is it your foot?" (I forgot to mention Racquel has two beautiful pale pink cheeks which stick out on her face like glacé buns; she gives an impression of iridescent good health.

"Yes, it is my foot." (How dare you woman me.) [And in my own house.]

"Twingeing a bit?"

"Twingeing like hell."

"Bad luck," says the B. joining in with a Bloaterism, a piece of false sympathy which allows him to follow up with what's really in his mind. He says it musingly:

"I went to the funeral of Prince Youssoupoff in Paris—on the way back."

"How interesting!" (That's Racquel.)

"Well, it *was*. But it was a very damp, gloomy day, and I'm afraid it brought on my catarrh."

"Is that *all* you can say about the funeral of the assassin of Rasputin?" (That's myself, very stinging. Luckily I saw the obituary in Th*e Times* on Friday, so I don't feel out of it.)

"I know what you mean," says the B., eager not to be on the wrong side of conventional feeling. He pauses out of respect for history. Then, like lightning, back to the catarrh. "But I shall have to do something about my sinuses. I can't risk getting them blocked like this." Blocked again!

He uncorks the thermos and firmly pours and drinks a cup of soup. It's tomato. I say absolutely nothing. I'm waiting for another "poor man" from Racquel.

Next the B. makes an inner laughing noise, and after a number of bright flirtatious glances in my direction says with shy whimsy:

"I hope you're not annoyed with me!"

"Tell me more about your catarrh."

"Min!" Racquel is very shocked. "He hasn't even had a chance to take his coat off!"

"Now you want him to undress! And a minute ago you said he was frozen."

"Well, I don't mind 'undressing' if you want me to."

He takes off his coat with a great deal of professional skill. If there was a male strip-tease, this is how it would start—with a red fur coat. Stripped down to his suit, he eyes us. Racquel seems to be dazed by it, while remaining chaste and nun-like. Is she storing away men in a man-bank before taking her final vows?

He swirls round suddenly and says to me in an intimate voice:

"I've been thinking a lot about you."

Flirting with me in front of Racquel! It's—immoral, like flirting with someone after you've just made love to them. But instead of saying: "Yeah?" like a coarse gouty television sheik, I find myself replying in a gentle tone:

"Have you, Carlos?"

"Yes." He nods across Racquel as if she didn't exist. She keeps very still, while he goes on casually:

"I've got two tickets for *Falstaff* Wednesday after next. Would you like to come?"

Normally I'd get up and go and look in my diary and hum and haw, and wonder if I could bear a whole evening alone with him, and finally say: "No, I'm working." But Racquel's presence is stimulating me to a degree. I can feel the price of flesh veering up and down. Billy's calm voice can't be heard against the ponderous male silence which the B. has created. If he crooked his finger at Racquel she'd lay her shining auburn head against his chest and get herself squeezed to death. She's really begging to be battered black and blue. I've got a feeling that if I say "No" he'll ask her, and she'll say "Yes" and they'll—

I get up in a sudden fit of rage which takes them both by surprise, and shout:

"All right! I'll go!"

"*Good.*" The B. instantly stands up as though a business deal has been put through. He whips his belongings together, glances at nothing, bends over Racquel for half a second's chocolate-box smiling, and is out of the front door, all power, cosmopolitanism, and unblocked lust. All the same, *Falstaff* is a rotten choice for a seduction, far too witty. All you can say is that at least he didn't choose *Fidelio.*

It's the Saturday after the Bloater's trap and I'm still raging about the house and going through imaginary scenes with him. I've decided to be polite and nasty and ask for food in *both the intervals.* No doubt the B. intends to melt me with music and hard liquor so that I end the evening like human mashed potato, all ready to be scooped into his arms. I do see that people with a gift for the obvious tend to win in life. Well, I'll soon put that right. Here's a dirty old envelope, just the thing to write him a note on. I write: "I say, Carlos, could I have chicken breast salad, thin brown bread and butter and some nice Alsatian wine in the first interval, and in the second real fruit salad with real cream, *petits fours* and Turkish coffee?" That ought to take up the slack in his mind and empty his wallet. Then I can stump about the opera house with my gouty foot, so seductive.

There's a ring at the front door, but I'm playing at being "out" ever since the B. trap, and ignore it. Another long strong bell noise. I go calmly into the bathroom and wash my hands. As soon as the soapy water disappears I remember that the waste pipe empties into a square drain with a grating over it, right beside the front door, so whoever is standing there will be looking at the same water going down with a gurgle, and will—Ah, just as I thought, an impatient hand is rattling the letter-box. Too fast for the B. It could be Claudi. Certainly not a woman, a peremptory rattle like that—well, perhaps a woman over fifty with a large patent leather handbag and four thousand a year.

I've taken the precaution of leaving open the front window of the spare room on the first floor. And I creep into the room and quickly put my head out. Damn! Not quick enough. A male head, not unlike Claudi's, looks up and starts interrogating me:

"Is that Mrs So-and-so?"

I frown; the parts of life connected with being Mrs So-and-so need care.

"Yes."

"I've got a painting for you."

"I haven't bought one." That comes out firmly!

"I know. This is a present from Mr Carlos Hamburger. May I bring it in?"

Another present from the B.! He must be ill. First the D'Annunzio, which he might at a pinch have come by from some aunt. But a painting! My strongest impulse is to send it away on the spot. Bang goes my chicken breast salad ordered on a dirty envelope. The B. is giving me unexpected, expensive things. He's disarming me. He's actually thinking what will give me pleasure; it's so—out of character. Anyway, if it comes to that, I'd far rather have a gramophone record. Surely he must know that? But of course he does! He's giving me something I don't particularly want, so that I'll feel uneasy and won't be able to toss off my orders and assert myself. I feel seriously weakened and thrown off balance; very nearly checkmated. I can see those *Falstaff* intervals will be filled by hard drink after all. I decide to play for time, and say feebly to the upturned head:

"Well, I've got rather a bad foot ..."

Obviously he's had people refusing paintings before because he seems to have expected my remark, and says:

"Well, perhaps I can hand it up to you. Then you won't have to come down. It's not very heavy."

How resourceful people are. It's infuriating. This man is quite definitely in the Claudi category. He's dragging the dustbin along beside the ground-floor window-sill as if born to it. And you know what a hideous noise grating dustbins make—screech, screech. There, he's got it right. And up he goes on the lid just like Charlie Chaplin. It's all turning into a typical Bloater situation, red fur coats, soup, catarrh, and grating dustbins.

"Can you reach?"

I'm definitely feeling sour. And here comes Claudi himself! And he's going to help. God, they're like two ablebodied grey-haired clowns together. Claudi says:

"What a charming painting. May I see it?"

"No, darling, I haven't seen it myself yet."

I stretch down, and my opponent stretches up, and when I've taken a grip on it, he says quickly:

"Oh be careful! It's still wet in places."

He reproaches me! And both my hands are covered with navy-blue paint. Too bad. It'll go into the cracks in my fingers and my nails will look like Claudi's after gardening. What else is on the canvas? A streak of red. That's wet too. The whole thing's like a well licked postage stamp, or a fly paper. Shall I hand it down to him again? Then he can pass it to Claudi, and we'll all be tarred with it. No wonder people loathe the arts; wet paintings and humming baritones. He's waiting for my exclamation of delight down there, he's got his head cocked all ready to catch it in his left ear. I intend to defeat him. I'm not going to be jogged into screams of joy by an art dealer on a dustbin lid. Especially when I started off by being "out." I say calmly:

"Is there a frame?"

"A frame? No!" That's a straight win for me. And now I've thought of something even better. But before I can say it, I must ruffle my hair and make a half-yawn like a little petted female who can't get through the morning without peppermint creams at eleven-thirty. Ready? Here it is:

"It looks expensive."

There's no answer to that and he climbs down to the ground, grim and shrunken. (Can you believe it!) I lean out and smile at him; I've got to smile now that the navy-blue paint is all over my hair. I'm balancing "I like it *terribly*" against "It really is good" but I can't decide which one is the more stupid. So I say:

"Sweet of you to bring it."

There's not an ounce of humour in him; I don't know why I even bother to send him up. Why do art dealers force one to extreme behaviour like this? I suppose after fifty you have to take it all seriously, and then you become an idiot. It's all very out of date.

He goes off, the perfect little Philistine aesthete, grumpy

shoulders braced to take the knocks. Still, there haven't been too many knocks, he's expensively dressed and if he can get money out of the Bloater for a wet navy-blue painting, he's not doing too badly.

Claudi thrives on all this. His eyes are like sparklers. He says in his coaxing way:

"Are you going to let me in, sweetie-pie? Now that you've got rid of my double!"

"So you noticed that!"

"I notice everything, my dear."

"I'm not really in a mood to be my-deared. I'm in grave danger."

"Again! This must be the sexiest house in London. A real *maison française*."

Without warning a tirade bursts out of me:

"Oh Claudi, how could you say that! If you knew what I wrote in my diary this morning, you'd be sorry. God, I feel so miserable and frustrated I'd like to lie down in some lousy stinking old Beckett play and just rot there. I hate men. I don't think they're men at all."

Claudi comes up very close below the window and fixes his eyes, taking away the sparkle and making them very blue and glowing.

"Sweetie-pie, if I were to tell you about the way women deceive men."

"Oh ho-ho-ho."

"Putting belladonna into their eyes to make their pupils larger. I tell you you go out after a woman in life and you buy her—"

"*Buy* her?"

"Yes, you buy her thinking you are getting a young Venus, and what happens? Her long false eyelashes come off and she has no eyes at all. Her hair, which looked blonde, is all grey at the roots. And you take her corset off and she has no bosom at all, nothing bigger than two little aspirin tablets, not even enough to catch hold of, and you are in a medieval landscape, back in the thirteenth century, with all your illusions gone."

"Claudi, will you please stop shouting."

"Men at least don't cheat like that. It's as though I went out," he's laughing but managing to hiss all this in a stage whisper, "and bought the biggest banana I could get hold of."

"Claudi, if you get rude, I'll close the window."

"Well, if you'd just come down like a nice little girl and open the door for me, we wouldn't have to have our private and intimate conversations in the street like this."

I go downstairs, still carrying the painting and reluctantly open the front door with my head on one side. Claudi, as usual, enters like a lemming making for the sea, that is to say, he gets in as far as possible and when he's about to hit his head on the opposite wall, he turns quickly and leans against it. Then he usually says "Ha," and sighs deeply.

Today, he looks at the painting (without touching it, I notice), and starts praising it up to the skies, as people do when they don't really care whether it's a painting or a brace of pheasants, but just want something to do.

"I tell you you are jolly lucky to get a little painting like that given to you."

"I don't want it," I say waspishly. "It's dirty."

"Sometimes, you know, Min, you make me feel very sad. No, honest to God, I really mean it."

"Claudi, you're shameless. You're as bad as the Bloater or worse. Do you know what this painting represents? A square meal and my honour." For a moment I really mean it, and then we both laugh much too noisily. After all, you can't play MacFisheries with a man and then go back to the prim and proper days as though nothing had happened.

Claudi, who knows everything, knew I'd get caught by the B. sooner or later but he wants detail, the avid little pest. I tell him a few things, and he asks:

"But Min, why did you say you'd go?"

I twist on the pin:

"Oh, I don't know. Racquel was sitting there in one of her blouses ..."

"I must meet this Racquel."

"Oh, she's more than a match for you. She's ginger."

Claudi puts on one of his considering-a-new-woman glances.

"Ginger—ah." He stretches. "Well, why not? If I can't have you, Min, I might as well have a ginger woman."

"Claudi, I do think we should clean up our conversations a little. It's twelve o'clock in the morning. It's not even tea-time."

"And who starts it all? I come in here, a decent well-respected elderly gentleman who wants to talk about his garden. And what happens? She gives me my orders. '*I want you to get rid of a Bloater*,' she says. '*Yes, madam, certainly, madam*,' I say, '*will that be all for today?*'"

"It's stale, darling. You've had the last little bit of juice out of it."

He turns on me, folds his arms, and takes up quite an angry attitude; then he says seriously and with force:

"The question is: do you want him or not?"

I'm not sure that I've heard properly. Claudi can certainly pull some direct questions out of the hat when he wants to. He goes on in a lower tone, but with plenty of bite:

"And if so, *how much* do you want him, Min, and for *how long?*"

Naturally I grind to a halt under this kind of attack. He's trying to get in among my thoughts before I've even thought them. I feel like wailing and falling down, but I can't get rid of my intelligent expression quickly enough. He's managed to turn the hall into a little law court, and he's having the time of his life, grilling me. I slide my eyes away and say inconsequentially:

"He takes his lucky piano stool with him in a taxi. It goes up and down with a horrid little pedal."

Claudi says involuntarily:

"That's enough to damn him for a start."

"That's better! You frightened me for a minute. So you see, darling, I know what Michal the daughter of Saul felt like when she saw David dancing about in front of the ark."

"What did she feel like?"

"Well, he stopped being masculine. The ark was a sort of lucky piano stool. As soon as men start dancing about and doing tricks and so on, you can't take them seriously."

"So you don't take him seriously?"

"Not for a moment. And anyway, he's in love with his catarrh. Just as you are with your garden."

"Min, I have told you before—"

"All right. Even if you're *not* in love with your garden, I still can't stand the Bloater. He's got flabby flesh."

"Well, Min," Claudi is sad and thoughtful, "we can't all be as hard as tennis balls."

This makes us laugh for nearly two minutes. By then I'm feeling relatively safe, and Claudi is back as an old friend and mainstay in whom I can confide. Still, just to clear the air of any lingering pro-Bloater atmosphere, I make a final gesture. Pointing to the telephone pad which is covered with scribblings, I say with a certain histrionic talent:

"Look at that!"

"What?" Claudi jumps on it and quickly reads up all my week's appointments, knowing there won't be a second chance like this in a lifetime.

"You see that doodling down the side there that goes on and on?"

"Yes, like knitting."

"That's *his*. Could anything be more boring?"

"Hmm. Hmm. Very regular. He keeps doing the same thing."

"Exactly. Hideous monotonous knitting. Just rows of it. Not very masculine, is it?"

I can see that Claudi now wants to show me *his* doodles; he picks up the pencil and thinks. I say:

"You're not allowed to think, darling. It's cheating."

He draws something carefully and gazes down at it, really interested. I look over his shoulder. He's drawn a sort of oval fried egg with a spike coming up out of it.

"Well done. It's faintly obscene."

He's pleased, and smiles to himself as though he's passed a test. At the last minute he feels that perhaps he should take an interest in my telephone doodles, and says half-heartedly:

"What do *you* do, Min?"

"Oh, I do a clock with no numbers and the hands wrenched out of it."

Without warning he decides to make capital out of this, and nods his head as though he's gained the ultimate clue to my character.

"You are a very, very strange woman, my dear child."

I'm furious. The ingratitude of it! I give him infinite pleasure by telling him he's done an obscene drawing, and in return he tells me I'm strange. I don't want to be strange, and I'm not going to let him get away with it.

"I'm not in the least 'strange.' I'm logical. Whereas you, Claudi dear, are absolutely *sui generis*. Sometimes it's too much for me." He makes an "Ooh!" of someone truly winded. "I feel I can't keep up with your dancing."

"Listen to it! First she gets rid of one man, and then she gets rid of another. And all because she says they're *dancing*. Oh you Michal the daughter of Saul!"

"Talking of dancing, you never even asked me how my poor old foot was."

Claudi bows his shoulders as though the burden on them is too great. He croaks:

"Stop. It's too much. I'm too old after all. Game, set, and match, my little Min. Now I'll just go home and look at my roses."

I feel mean, and take a step towards him, uttering a peace-making sentence:

"Would you like me to come and look at them for you, darling?"

"No thank you, sweetie-pie. Last time you looked at your wrist-watch before sniffing the floribundas."

When he's gone, I'm left with the dirty envelope in one hand and the painting in the other. It's a toss-up. I start humming a melodious piece of musical cross-talk from *Falstaff*. I know the opera backwards, and when some of the chief characters come in together in Scene II and sing against one another in a scurrying egocentric counterpoint, everyone in the audience smiles involuntarily. Such vanity, such worldiness, such *fun*, just like oneself. Yes, the last time I felt this kind of stifled mirth was at school when we stole trifle from the kitchens in a bucket for a midnight feast. But can you imagine the B. …? Yes, I can.

7

Jenny is going to make herself ill over the guitar. This afternoon, for instance, she's so lackadaisical, I tried to cheer
her up by playing through the Orestes poem and saying
loudly "That's good" every time we came to a piece of
sound she'd made, but she wouldn't respond. And that sort
of behaviour is catching. Look at Fred, he's so slumped he
looks like a pilot who's been in the cockpit for forty-eight
hours. In that mood he'll take exception to anything. And
this studio is so *brown,* brown carpet, speakers with brown
woven radio-set material over their mouths. There's too
much negative irritation about. That's because the sounds
plunge you rapidly from elation headlong into depression.
We all get quarrelsome as though we're looking for water
in a desert. Or just firm ground.

"You'll never get that heart-beat to sound like a heart-
beat," says Fred, the defeatist.

"So what? It's a real heart-beat. It was recorded in hospital. It's the real thing." I'm trying, at least.

Jenny says petulantly:

"I don't think it's normal. It sounds as though it's got
heart disease."

"Yes," says Fred, siding with her, "it sounds like an old
blackbird flapping a pair of rotten wings."

The ranks are closing against me, and at any moment a
serious discussion of work will turn into chatter. Someone

puts their head round the studio door and says: "Sorry." Jenny and Fred look up with hope. I keep staring at my music-stand with ridges on my brow, praying the interruption won't rend the veil of the temple from top to bottom.

Actually, they're too apathetic to take advantage of it. Fred plays with his tools, a razor, a miniature screwdriver, and some joining tape. He wants to make *his* heart-beat, and that will take at least three-quarters of an hour. If it's better than the one I've brought in from outside, from the sound library, I can use it. If it's worse, we shall have to start at this point all over again tomorrow morning. And if you stick in one place too long in constructing electronic sounds, you lose your ear, your memory of sound already used, and your ability to improvise spontaneously so that the whole thing "jells." Fred says:

"At the moment it sounds like bad Boulez."

I'm careless and take the bait.

"God, I think all Boulez sounds like bad Boulez. What a conventional musical brain!"

"There's nothing wrong with a conventional musical brain," says Fred, who has one, "that's where you begin."

Now I'm for it. He's going to bring out his few platitudes and dust them in public. In no time at all I'll become another Fred because any discussion of basic truths has a levelling effect and you lose your imaginative queenship or kingship at the double. Look at Oxford Street—a street full of pawns if ever there was one; try standing there and calling out "Master!" Not a soul would turn round. (A "*Cher Maître!*" in the Boul Mich would be very different.)

"A sound knowledge of the conventions—" says Fred, winning and ageing at the same moment.

"Should be disguised after the age of seventeen." I'm talking just as he intended, and he nods to keep me going.

I feel my Fredship beginning; a feeling that I've just put on an overcoat made of lead. "Well, possibly Boulez is cleverer than I think. But why does he talk such tripe?"

Of course this is blasphemy and they both look at me as if I've spoken during the two-minute silence on Armistice Day. Fred alone is able to put his finger on one of those far-cical modern boredoms by which critics "explain" things:

"Well, to begin with, you must consider the level of musical and general education of the average audience to which he ..."

Don't worry. In spite of everything, I'm still inhumanly human. At the sound of "to which he" I come to myself. My Fredship goes up in a clap of thunder. I say with reck-less wickedness:

"'*To which he*' is perfect, honestly. I want '*to which he*' in letters of gold on my tomb. I've given up my whole life to '*to which he.*' Fred, you're a genius because without you I should never have discovered it. You've put bureaucracy in a nutshell."

He hasn't caught on and is still, in a dazed way, trying to finish that impossible sentence. I've done an unforgivable thing, of course. When he wakes up to the insult there will be murder. Jenny warns me, just saying "Take care!" with those famous green marbles nearly out on stalks. There's no help for it; if I don't act *at once* the resentment will last for weeks and my programme will be ruined. So I take the expedient which is lying handy.

"Fred, that heart-beat—sorry to interrupt what you were saying, I tend to go off the point (like hell)—would you have a go at making another heart-beat for me? If it wouldn't take too long?"

He gets up, still dazed, but interested. Will he put that wordy little flight of mine down to eccentricity? If he does, we're saved (apart from the waste of three-quarters of an hour). But if he turns it over in his mind, if he penetrates past the words to the meaning, he'll probably refuse to work with me. He'll strangle me. He'll throw his tea-break over me. And I shall never make him understand that my comments weren't personal, but merely diabolical! Oh Fred, I almost feel tenderness for you, when I realise how disinterested it was, that piece of wickedness! All the same, better keep talking.

"The moment you've recorded it, could you let me hear it, Fred? Really loudly, so that I can compare it with the first?"

"I think Fred's right about Boulez." Jenny is indeed a very clever girl. The note of approval in her voice and those words spoken at exactly the right moment, have a nourishing effect. Fred receives them on his neck, sideways, and goes peacefully about his task. What she says to me in dumb-show is: "You idiot! What did you do that for? Hurting his feelings! All for nothing! And here am I, dying to get away to my guitar!"

The moment he's out of the studio, and the silencing, padded door swings shut, Jenny says as a comment on the whole incident:

"Miaou!"

"No!" I say sternly. "Be fair. He ought to consider my feelings, too. Aren't I supposed to have any feelings?"

"Well, you're giving the orders, so he's going to play at being a technician." Jenny is accurate as usual.

"On the continent in electronic studios enthusiastic young people *with ideas* work together as a team." My chin lifts as I speak.

"And look what they produce!"

"And the hoo-ha they talk about it."

We both have a picture of flashy continental composers in white macs, young, clean-shaven, and curt in speech, arriving at London Airport with pamphlets and lectures in bison-skin despatch-cases. Whereas here we are, sitting about, waiting for a left-wing bureaucrat with no imagination to make a heart-beat. I say morosely:

"It's their broken English. They're pure Fred underneath."

"Tell that to the music critics here."

She starts pulling at her hair and winding it along a finger. Then she lets it go, puts some ends in her mouth and bites them. She looks at me.

"Jenny!"

"I'm having terrible nights," she says timidly.

"Alone?"

"Yes, of course alone. It's hell."

"But you were sleeping so well. I could hardly bear it."

"Well, I'm not now. The other night I woke up and didn't know where I was. I felt I was upside down somehow."

"*You*, Jenny, the practical one with hundreds of spare men."

"You the married woman with a husband in a husband-bag!" Jenny mimics my way of phrasing things in a way I don't much like. She needs putting right on married life. I say sombrely:

"You can have terrible nightmares with a man lying beside you in bed. Especially if he's your husband. If anything it makes it worse. Because you're chained there, not allowed to move. And they rove about, you know. Sometimes they climb mountains and then hang on the tops by their fingernails—and wake up all white and gasping in the morning. And sometimes they leap like salmon. And they *all* twitch."

I gaze back at her, complacent, the wronged wife. She's not a bit interested, and goes on about her nightmare:

"I found myself out of bed, absolutely lost, in total darkness. So I groped about and came to a door and opened it—"

"And found yourself in the clothes cupboard nearly smothered by a lot of coats."

"Yes, how did you know?"

"I've done it a hundred times." (I remember doing it once when I was about seven.) But nothing can stop Jenny today, and she says:

"Well, after getting out of that lousy cupboard, I tried to find my bed again."

"Oh, that's hopeless."

"What do you do, then? Stay out there all night? No, I reasoned it out: if I can find the cupboard, I can find my bed. Q.E.D." (Poor old Jenny, she really is rambling on. And this is all the work of *one* guitar). I say quite kindly:

"And did you find it? I suppose you must have done or you wouldn't be here."

"Min, do you know I searched for it for *hours*. It's the most horrible feeling, being lost and trying to find your bed. I'd almost given up ... you know, I was on my knees going over every foot of the floor area ..."

"Oh Jenny!" For the first time I really am shocked. The thought of her being brought to her knees sickens me.

"And then I found it!"

"Well, thank God for that."

"Or rather I found the end of the bed. But I wasn't in a mood to quibble."

"No fear!"

"So I climbed up over the headboard thing and got in that way. Boy, what a relief! I was never so pleased to get anywhere in all my life. I just lay there, smiling fatuously."

"It almost sounds worth the exercise. But life shouldn't be like this!"

I've just made a powerful remark, and we both know it. Jenny suddenly shakes out all her hair loosely, and then combs it through with two combs made of her stiffened fingers. She smiles for apparently no reason, but I know why. And says:

"Of course it shouldn't. What one needs is a four-poster bed, ample and sweet-smelling. You draw the curtains and look across to the opposite pillow—and there—"

I have, at this moment, a really terrible vision of the Bloater. I shiver, and quickly replace it with—with Billy! Yes, there he is on the opposite pillow, looking much younger, no divorce marks on his face, passionate, calm, attentive ... and with that skin of his brewed in Jermyn Street, that rose-coloured masculine skin. And on his chest? I have to stop. Is there, or is there not, hair? I say abruptly:

"Has he got hair on his chest, Jenny?"

She answers without hesitation:

"No. It's more or less smooth. He adores it when I stroke him. He lies quite still for me to do it, but never for too long. He's too good a lover for that. Under that white skin, he's bound together with muscle like an eel. From the moment he begins to make love, he literally cannot stop. He's caught by his own skill. He says it's because I'm irresistible."

"Does he stop to answer the telephone?"

"He unplugs it the moment I arrive."

"So you *have* made love to him!"

"Nearly. But not quite." She's teasing me.

"What does 'not quite' mean?"

Jenny becomes quiet, and says almost modestly:

"Not quite, Min dear, means I won't take off all my clothes. Only the top half."

"And he ...?" I have to know, for the sake of my own future.

"He—has undressed. He wants me to know what he looks like."

"My God, it sounds like a fight to the death." (And *you* want him to know what you look like.)

"Sometimes I think I could resist him, if it weren't for his mouth which tastes and smells so perfect. You know, everything begins with the mouth."

"Does it? Oh. And his ..."

"Is like fresh, hot water. And the awful thing is, Min, once you're hooked on one mouth, you can't bear all the others. You look at them and you think: 'No, wrong shape, not intelligent enough.'"

"You don't think you'll get bored with the same mouth kissing you in the same way, night in, night out?"

Jenny shakes her head violently, and groans forth:

"That's what I used to think! This one, I used to think, accompanied by a moustache, will be more interesting than that one, which is too *etched-in*—you know what they say, a kiss without a moustache is like a boiled egg without salt."

"But surely a connoisseur like you is bound to get bored sooner or later with just one, clean-shaven mouth?"

"No, never! Never! I'm hooked. It's terrible. And I don't know *why.*"

I've never seen anyone look so forlorn. It seems to be up to me to change the direction of the conversation, because she really is suffering. I'm beginning to feel almost magnanimous. I count up my men, and smugly put a rubber band around them. But of course only Racquel knows the prices on the male stock-exchange. I feel it's now up to me to contribute some information for the general store. So I say:

"Did you know that men are terrified of women with sensuous mouths? I found out last week."

"Yes, of course," says Jenny stuffily.

"Oh." I'm stumped, and venture to ask: "Why?"

"Because they're scared they won't come up to expectation. They reason it like this: if a woman has a sensuous mouth, she'll make huge demands and expect me to do the Indian rope trick at least. This frightens me to death, so I'll keep off and find someone a bit prim. Then I can blaze away like a fire-cracker."

I can't help giving her an admiring glance. She says:

"The beastly thing about sex is the steady, relentless gloom of the men. They just lose all sense of humour."

"They just go bad."

"They have to be controlled."

"They ought to read that bit in the *Kama-Sutra* where it says: 'When a courtesan gets to the end of her tether she should gather up all the loot, all the objects, and in a low, growling voice expel her lover from her bed.'"

"Aren't you paraphrasing it a bit?"

"Well, possibly. Just a bit."

Jenny says with real longing:

"The *Kama-Sutra* does simplify life. Shall we go to India?"

"Good idea. And there are *hundreds* of them over there."

We feel rich and fortified. The atmosphere relaxes.

"By the way, Jenny, how's your burn?"

"So-so. I have to keep going to hospital to get it dressed. But it's almost been worth it for the surgeons."

"That's more like the old Jenny!"

She laughs slightly, and asks after my gouty foot.

"My old foot? It's like your burn, it depends entirely on the doctors. At the moment I've been down to a horribly expensive one who only examined my chest."

"That's a promising start. Is he French?"

"Nearly. I feel the word '*suppositoire*' is only just round the corner. But I really can't afford him. So I've got to get better."

Thinking back over this conversation later, I decided that Jenny has a great deal of style when it comes to answering awkward questions. Lots of women dive down and pull out some pretty repellent descriptive phrases when it comes to admissions about their private lives. But Jenny always keeps it light and cool. "Only the top half" may be an ordinary schoolgirl's phrase, but you should hear what some women would substitute for it. Racquel, for instance, without uttering a word is somehow—basic. And anyway I can just hear her saying: "I stripped to the waist. It was my duty for a man of genius." What is she up to? Shall I give her the Bloater? Shall I? Or, just a minute, what about my dear, darling, good, lovable George? Is he getting his fair share of Life? Or is he right now putting in for a couple of outright pornographic books at the B.M. just to get through the afternoon? But if I find her sinister, wouldn't he find the same? No, he's a man; he'll see it all from a different angle. I know what. Claudi must be the test case. He must spend a whole tea-time bottled up with her. I'll leave them together in the sitting-room. Now Claudi gets bored very easily. If he comes away raving, it means she's not boring and not sinister. In which case it's my absolute duty to save George from that horrible porno at the B.M. But I mustn't let him see Racquel sewing. As soon as George sees a woman doing a domestic task he feels trapped, as though she's trying to build a house up round him and stabilise him. In fact, he's static to a degree. But he doesn't want the point to be rammed home. What he wants is a thoroughly dangerous woman, a Jezebel, home-breaker, snake-pit belly dancer—in a sophisticated form, and dressed in the height of fashion of course. God, life is tiring.

I may say that when Fred came back with his heartbeat, we were both in such a good humour that I very nearly put it in. The danger is that I shall get fond of him if he goes on letting me insult him, and we'll end up doing the programme his way. "*To which he, to which he,*" it's like St Vitus's dance, once you start saying it you can't stop. Jenny does it in the form of an owl noise when we meet. Fred's had far more attention since he said that than he's ever had in his life before. Jenny told him she'd seen a purple tie which would suit him to a tee. And I gave him my last Gauloise, and laughed at one of his jokes when I was in a hurry, really late, to see Billy.

8

Never mind French doctors, there's an avenue leading up to Hampstead Heath which really is French. Whitish. Plane trees with patches on the trunks come straight out of the tarmac walk (that's blue and humped) and join twenty feet aloft—the same height as the stained glass windows in Gerona cathedral. You get your daylight stained green or amber but always with rose in it, due to the flush that lies over London on a good September afternoon. All those plate-glass windows down there behind you throw up a pink sky from three o'clock. And the man treading firmly up the path beside you is, if you are lucky ... Billy!

We go through the leaves together, not bothering to talk. Our feet are scrunching things up; and in a moment or two we shall look at one another to find out how far we've got. But just now we're enjoying the new dimension we've added to our relationship with this daylight *rendezvous.* How did it come about? Two diehard metropolitans taking an afternoon off and walking under *trees*? And I used to be the sort of person who could only take a walk down the Charing Cross Road and then only at certain times of the day when I knew I'd meet someone I know and be interrupted. Ah, I can just hear the distant klaxon of the police cars. Thank God there's trouble somewhere.

These wooden seats have been carved to pieces by lovers. I respect the quickly scratched initials, which suggest that things are going well. But the ambitious calligraph is out; what it really says is: "Help! I'm carving my tombstone."

No, we're still not looking at one another. This slight awkwardness is most pleasant. Billy's shoulder, the one nearest to me, is much more powerful and attractive by day. The tweed coat he's wearing is almost a hacking jacket. I must say rough outdoor clothes have a physical power which is the equal of an animal's coat. Am I suitably dressed for this avenue of terracotta light? I've got some extremely expensive brown wool stockings on, and my skirt cuts them at thigh level; this gives me a rounded but delicate leg, and I rather fancy myself running along a skyline in them at top speed.

Billy has a naturalness about him which is breathtaking. For instance, I know that at any moment now he'll seek my hand and hold it. And we'll walk along like two contented children. I'll begin to chatter about the old days in Paris, or my school, or the Bloater ... oh, I don't know, about anything young, haphazard and amusing. Billy will listen, smiling and admiring me. His regard from those hazel eyes of his is always steady and interested, and his step is light and quick, just like my own, with the indiarubber spring in it suppressed for the sake of decency. The only thing about him which unsettles me is the delicate finish of his fingers. I once said to him:

"I'm afraid your fingers ... are cruel."

He was completely disconcerted, and looked at them as though they'd signed away all his money.

"Cruel, are they? What makes you say that?"

"I'm sorry. I was just speaking out carelessly. It's just the fastidious moulding of the tops of the fingers that frightens me."

"It frightens me too, now you've told me about it. Shall I change them?"

"No! And besides big, flat, obtuse male fingers wouldn't do for me at all."

Still, he never quite got over it. And even now he'll look down at them, and then glance up at me enquiringly. "Cruel, are they? Shall I change them?"

Billy's head is so intelligent it doesn't seem to matter that it hasn't any especial feature to which one can point and say: "Look at that curly brown hair" or "What a manly nose, what thickets of eyebrows!" There's not a moment when it isn't giving out life, restraining its humour and emotions, perfectly at ease with itself. I have this tendency to boil down my whole past life into a sort of pure beef essence before I can begin anything new. But Billy moves straight into the future without effort. In fact he's one of the few people who are simultaneously alert to their own past, present, and future.

We've come to a crossroads. One path slopes down between the fishing ponds.

"This way," says Billy, taking my hand.

Oh, what a warm, nervous, knowledgeable hand. I trot beside him like a little girl. No need to look at one another now, we are in complete harmony.

The path is lined with boys fishing. The water is just as it should be, full of moods. Down at the edge here it's a transparent brown sugar aquarium with fudge-coated leaves at the bottom. Over there, it's impenetrable, white, glossy, and the fishing lines go into it at an angle and disappear. The smell of freshwater is so new.

"Mind your eyeballs as we go through them, Billy! They can't cast for toffee nuts, but they're really good at hooking out the eyeballs of people on the path."

He minds his eyeballs, and we hurry through.

"Here's the kite-flying hill, Billy. Isn't it lovely!"

"Lovely!"

"Look at all these dogs, they're so big. God, I loathe them."

"Do you loathe them, Min?" asks Billy, with a genuine wish to know.

"Of course. I loathe them because they're big. They ought to be in cages. Look at that one, it's the size of a human being. And they're sexless, almost, it's fantastic. You never see two of them ... Well, anyway, it's a good thing because we don't want them to reproduce themselves. I tell you, Billy, all these dogs care about is meat, walks, master, and barking loudly. They're the most bourgeois eunuch dogs in the world."

"And they all seem to be the same colour ..."

"Yes, like pease pudding. Except for the black ones."

"It might be different if we got to know them," says Billy temperately.

"Do I lose marks for not being a dog-lover?"

"You know perfectly well that in England, only in England, you gain full marks for not being a dog-lover. Actually, you rather like them, Min. If you saw a little dog that took your fancy you'd go straight up and talk to it. It's just that you treat them as you treat strange human beings."

"How do I treat you, Billy?"

"I'm not sure yet. But I'm a Min-lover, so it doesn't really matter." He puts a little pressure on my hand and his eyes are brightly lit and tender.

"Billy, you make the sky bluer."

"So do you."

Dare we stop and embrace? It's a rotten place. On the side of a hill, with no cover, not even a scruffy little bush.

And here come two panting runners in blue track-suits! We walk on up the hill pondering it, that embrace which we put aside for the moment. I decide to ask obvious, awkward questions.

"Billy, what was your motive in coming out with me to-day?"

"I wanted to walk beside you in the fresh air, and just listen to you talking about things."

"You make me so interested in myself! But seriously ... I've got this tendency to tremble, Billy. It worries me. Anything new or strange, or you, and lo and behold I tremble."

"I know. I love it. I want you trembling in my arms."

"Oh, Billy!"

I'm flabbergasted. It's a complete emotional scoop. But for the forward action of our walk, I'd probably fall down. I say in a low voice:

"Why do you say things like that? It's so frightening."

"I'm glad. I meant it to be."

Now we can never go back, and we both know it. When we get to the bottom of the hill and reach that little group of trees, Billy will kiss me. And I shall begin to think, and to long, and to be jealous. My peace of mind and my gaiety will be gone for ever. I shall have to be balanced and to keep my heart strong, to fight and to be catty, and to re-invent my arrogance all over again by an effort of will. It's almost too much. My much prized, friendly, reliable Billy will turn into a male whose flesh will keep me awake at night, and I shall have no one to phone up and complain to when he makes me unhappy. It really is the limit. I say sharply:

"Do you want to see my favourite places on the Heath, or *don't* you?"

"I do. Of course."

"Do you want me to whistle a theme from *Trovatore* while standing on that old tree-trunk, or *not*?"

"Yes, I'll lift you up."

"*I don't want to be lifted up yet.*"

He waits to see how I shall protect myself in the next few minutes. He knows I'll invent tirelessly all the way down the side of the hill, so as to make myself too weak to resist him at the bottom. Everything I do or say will hurt and please him. I say nastily:

"Do you want to hear what the Bloater did the very last time I was in a restaurant with him?"

"What?"

"He ordered jugged hare, and it took *ages*. In the end I couldn't stand it any longer so I said: 'Your jugged hare is holding us up. It can't be my trout or George's mussels, so it's your stupid jugged hare. And anyway, it's not hare at all these days, it's cat. So if you swallow a bit of fur-coat, it's pussy.' And, Billy, you know what makes me rage? He laughed as though it was funny, when it wasn't. I know when I'm making a joke and when I'm just making conversation."

"Yes, that's terribly annoying."

"One jugged hare after another. And what good does it do him?"

"Obviously very little."

We're nearly at the bottom of the hill, so naturally I'm getting more and more petulant and spiteful. I stamp on the ground and want everything. I must touch him on a raw edge before we reach the trees. I'm taking revenge, you see, already, for all the suffering which is to come.

"I hope," my voice at its most exquisite, frozen and bitchy, "you're not making the mistake of thinking you can sum me up?"

Billy frowns very quickly, but it's only a thoughtful frown. Suddenly he takes my other hand in his empty one and holds each separately, so that we have to come slowly to a halt. I say:

"Gosh, what an excellent way to hold hands. No one would ever think you'd had a divorce."

The trees are over us, and I cry out desperately:

"Billy, winter's coming and *I don't like it.*"

"No, darling, but I'm here."

I'm here. What a lie. It's started already. What's the use of being amusing, when it's all going to end with a moan and my head laid submissively under his chin?

At first when his mouth touches mine, he kisses almost badly, not a seeking kiss, not a careful well-educated movement, and I think with real despair: "Good heavens, that's the worst first kiss I've ever had." Also he astounds me by taking his mouth away, just long enough to look at me closely and say "Isn't it like Chez Victor's?" (the restaurant where we've dined so often).

Then he begins to kiss with closed lips the corners and the middle of my mouth. He opens my mouth with a timing and sensibility so like my own that I get lost—what's happened? I'm not the spectator I'm accustomed to being; I'm not in front of him, nor am I getting left behind. At the split second this occurs to me, Billy puts both his arms round me, grips closely, and his mouth begins to force and take with the greatest possible skill and passion. A cold wind touches our faces, the illusion of freedom, the open air, the ebbing of my fears, the harmonious force and movement of our warm heads—all combine to ideal forgetfulness, joy, and desire.

In a minute I wake up. I'm going to talk and torment him.

"Billy!"

"Min." He goes over my eyebrows and my temples. He's capable of placing in the same spot, slowly, seven or eight entirely different kisses, dry, moist, affectionate, tender, seething, dominating, fraternal, and a healing, signing-off kiss on top.

We forget as we go on kissing one another that the effects are cumulative. It's simply banking up a great fire which is going to last all the winter, at least. We break off at the same moment, smiling and overjoyed. What friends! It's a disaster. Oh, I'd rather have an enemy any day. Billy says:

"Shall I lift you up now?"

I know it'll be dangerous, so I say at once:

"Of course."

He lifts me and swings me against him. Then he clasps his arms strongly so that I slide very slowly down inside them to my feet. Oh, what a calculating minx I am, and what a well-designed male slide that is, that allows me to fall so slowly that I can hardly bear it, and feel faint on the way down, so that when my mouth is level with his, I'm done for again. How grown-up we are this time and how fearless. Surely we'll be arrested for this sliding embrace. I, personally, can't stand it. I choke out:

"Tea! I must have tea and cake."

"Straight away?"

"Yes. Absolutely. I must."

I've got a good idea what I look like, no make-up, bruised mouth, lumpy marks on chin. When I think I'm looking ugly I always run very fast to get rid of it. Billy seems to sense this as I pull away from him. We run together and I'm instantly out of breath, and get a stitch. Billy manages to run without being ridiculous. I can hear something clinking in his pockets, though. Luckily he has the sense not to try to overtake me, so that I can stop, with a vague feeling that I've won, and don't have to go on and on.

"Have I won?" I ask imperiously.

"Oh yes. Long ago."

"Oh well, that's all right then," I say without hope.

I'm gloomy, and don't want to talk to anyone. Plim-Plam strolls through the house. Well, let it. Claudi took it off to the vet to get its teeth cleaned. The vet drugged it, poor thing, and then polished all its teeth. As soon as it came round it began eating; its appetite is like a lion's, and with all those sparkling white teeth the food disappears quick as a flash. The only trouble is, it won't put its tongue in. It's quite a pleasant little tongue, but the fact is, it's out. Claudi doesn't feel it's decent and is a bit upset. He follows Plim around, and when it sits down he rushes up and pokes its tongue in. "*In,* darling. Go in," he says. I'm in no mood for this sort of thing, and flash my cold glances to left and right.

I need new clothes. Something in P.V.C. with a vizor. I want to change the shape of my face, it should be absolutely round. Yes, I need a circular chin and a rosebud mouth to cope with Billy. And ten hours' sleep every night and a complete "don't care" kit of cigarettes, records, hairdressing appointments, films, and so on. Once I've decided on that, I realise it isn't enough. Even if I cram every hour of the day with phony pleasures I can't get rid of the smell of Billy's face, or of the authority and care of his arms when they grip me. Two thousand cucumber sandwiches, a Ferrari, a summer, raspberry jelly, ping-pong, a naked picnic in long grass, might possibly take my mind off him. One has to admit he knows how to woo. Oh God, why doesn't he make a few mistakes? He's bound to, sooner or later; you bet he's got some dancing routine hidden away, some David-in-front-of-the-ark caper that will really let him down. And I shall pounce on it without mercy. At all costs I must go on being spoilt and petted. I need *presents*.

Well, there's the D'Annunzio first edition and the painting, two of the most unsatisfactory presents I've ever had, intellectual hard cash. A compliment to my *mind*, simply asinine: D'Annunzio can't write and won't think for a start. Still, I like the green ribbons. No, I want something I can eat or wear or go to bed with—(Billy!). Yes, I'm ungrateful, impossible to please, inhuman, malicious, and demanding. Good! It's the only way to fight Billy. I've started gliding about the house practising the way I'm going to look up at him next time we meet; in height he's just about level with the coats hanging up in the hall. I give them my sparkling practice-glance. Not bad! And then a really wicked little squib of a smile, on and off in a flash. What a waste for a lot of overcoats! I might as well use it up on the Bloater.

My poor old Bloater, with your fifty or sixty unblocked successes! Why aren't you any good at seducing me? It's so easy. At least it seems to be. Have I got a roving eye, I wonder? How I hope I have!

Out of the blue I quickly pile up all my hair on top of my head and fix it with one sumptuous gesture, as though I've been doing it all my life. Then I pick a gigantic pink rose from the bunch Claudi brought me and fix it, all wet, at the summit. I look at myself in the mirror. What am I capable of? Almost anything today. "Mademoiselle Min, *grande horizontale* of the gout culture, needs Monsieur Billy, the amber musicologist, for a long, refreshing wooing with a happy ending." If you put that on the sleeve of a record it would sell out. I float my head to and fro in the mirror until I get tired of it. I'm looking at my reflection but in my inner ear I can just hear Jenny saying something funny: ("You know there are men who want to cut off their right hands to prove their love, when there is absolutely no necessity!")

Claudi seems to know there's been a change in my metabolism. He furbishes himself up more than ever, and keeps calling. Sometimes he says: "I'm protecting you from yourself, Min." He's fretting for his tea at the Ritz, but I obstinately refuse to go. Haven't time at the moment; it'll take me too far away from my thoughts—of Billy. "Anyway, the Waldorf is the place for tea," I say to him, and I'm heartily shocked to hear myself double-crossing him.

"But you said the Ritz!" says Claudi, knowing I've broken the code of honour.

"I know I said the Ritz. But you don't want me to keep my word, do you? The only thing that keeps me healthy and young is my dishonesty."

"Nonsense. You are the most trustworthy woman I know."

"I'm *not* going to the Ritz."

Claudi makes a circular promenade of the rug he's standing on, saying:

"If you were not a very a-ttt-ra-c-tive woman with a really superb figure—"

"The Waldorf."

"But at the same time a very snappy, really a thoroughly evil-tempered little bitch—"

"And when George makes a noise these days and irritates me, I don't hesitate to go downstairs and shout 'Bang, bang, bang!'"

"No, you don't hesitate to make a perfect little bitch of yourself." He seems to be quivering as though he's on fire. Is there nothing he won't do to draw attention to himself? He's pretending to be really angry. After all we've been through together! His cheeks are roasting hot, and there are far too many veins at the front of his neck.

I touch his coat.

"Do be careful, darling. Or I'll have to cool you down with a watering can."

He sulks and roasts, looks at the ground like a ten-year-old, and mumbles out some more mischief:

"You don't care about anybody these days, Min. You are getting so wrapped up in yourself, you just don't give a damn. Do you know you nearly lost your poor old friend the other day?"

He comes up close and makes the expression of a crazily faithful sheepdog; he practically sticks his tongue out like Plim-Plam.

"Did I, darling? How was that?"

"I had to go away for the weekend, and I couldn't get a taxi, so I tried to park on King's Cross Station ..."

Claudi really is unscrupulous. He's actually gone to the trouble of inventing an emotional situation so that he can cram down my throat some boring old parking story. And it was only yesterday he made me look up Cadogan Street for him, so that he could force an opportunity to enjoy his "parking and suffering" routine well in advance.

"... I'd no sooner stopped the car, just to take my bearings, when a policeman put his head in at the window and said: 'You can't stop here.'"

"Just a minute!" I raise my hand in imitation of such a policeman holding up the traffic. "*You*, Claudi, would not have the barefaced cheek ... to dare to tell me the story of how you got a parking ticket? You wouldn't darling, would you? Because if so, I shall stop believing in human nature."

He stops. His expression is now even more comical. The parking ticket story is waiting to be born, lying just inside his lips, and has obviously, I would judge from his eager manner, been there for quite some time. And since he hasn't been able to get rid of it on anyone else it must be a thing with overwhelming boredom value. I shudder.

From his scarlet countenance and his animated lips you can see his guilt laid bare. Finally he gabbles out what is obviously the end of a hellishly long zig-zag story:

"They towed it away to Waterloo Pound and the keys were still at the bottom of the lift-shaft!"

I smile with a mock sweetness I haven't felt since Billy kissed me, and say cheerfully:

"Well, thank God I nipped that in the bud."

Claudi, in order to justify himself, shouts:

"You're going off with your Bloater!"

"Well, you didn't make a very good job of getting rid of him!"

"You didn't want me to. I was obeying your unspoken wishes, the secret desires of your bosom."

"Claudi, you've got your tongue out just like Plim-Plam!"

"Yes, my dear, I'm slavering with lust like your great big baritone."

"Ah, my beautiful baritone!"

"So that's the way it goes?"

"With his panache what else can you expect?"

"What goes on inside that little pink and white porcelain face of yours, Min, I shall never know. Either you are the most terrible female plotter I have ever met, or else you're just a little schoolgirl chattering away about things she doesn't understand."

9

It's to be salmon and champers in the intervals. As for the
Bloater, he's never been so sizzling. He arrives dressed to
the nines. A trans-continental dinner jacket, a soft white
shirt with the most complex crimping down the front (almost a doily) edged in black. A purple tie, a purple silk
handkerchief in pocket—both flat and immaculate, or are
my eyes deceiving me? An opera cloak, lined again with
purple. His hair combed and scented, both glossy *and*
crisply curling (tongs?). Gloves, the score (in case I should
want it), a box of liqueur chocolates, naturally, to increase
drunkenness, a single red rose on a very long stalk, for me.
And on top of this, his hugeness all controlled, he moves
properly on clean, shiny shoes. Why, one could actually
take such a supple man skating!

Billy, *where are you?*

And the B. is holding right at the tips of his clean fingers
the scrumpled envelope I sent him with my menu for the
evening written down in terse badly formed writing.

Does he think I shall be embarrassed by this? No, no.
He's grown up in the last few months. He's at pains to explain to me the subtle reasons for countermanding certain
of my orders.

"I remembered," the massive, now scented head is bend-
ing down, "how much you liked smoked salmon. You used
to say you could stay up all night eating it."

"And that's exactly what I'm going to do."

"You made me laugh, you know, describing yourself sitting up in bed squeezing lemon over it while you read *War and Peace*."

"Well, bad luck. Because I'm not going to eat it in bed."

"Ha-ha-ha. No, of course not."

"Hee-hee-hee. You're dead right I'm not."

As for myself, I'm dressed in black, as if for a smart funeral, Prince Youssoupoff's perhaps. Except that I'm a trifle naked. Oh yes, even though the nakedness is down to the minimum, the B. keeps taking a deep breath as though he's doing the crawl and has to hurry because he's out of his depth. My dress is a very short pleated culotte in crêpe with a deep V neck, the skirt is two-thirds up my thigh and I've polished my legs with cream to make them shine. But really it's my feet that the B.'s eyes keep returning to. It's those vulgar sandals with imitation precious stones on them, they make my toes look straight and pretty. Is it that? No, it's the fact that they're *bare*. Bare feet, you understand, bare feet in Europe in late autumn are worth twenty-hundred-weight of *K. Sutras*. Don't think for a minute I've done this purposely. On the contrary, if I'd known the consternation they were going to cause I'd have worn gumboots. If the B. thinks that a pair of bare feet will be the supports for No. 61, then he can take those greedy, restless eyes off to the steppes of Russia for all the good his glaring and staring will do him.

Whew! He does believe in swivelling about. I've never been so out-Bloatered. What is that eau-de-cologne? He whooshes it this way and that, and it seems to flow out of his once-pestilential armpits in great waves of musty rain. I'm nearly asphyxiated, but one must admit it's good. I've just remembered Claudi's description of his coat, the old one lined with fur: "It smells as if it came off a dead Russian lance corporal." Come to think of it, tonight's smell is rather Russian. It smells like the old Czars' St Petersburg, pulverised at the height of its glory, and sold off in ounces of solid cologne ... one gets an impression of chandeliers, ice-buckets, and indoor Russians in crocodile shoes talking French.

Suddenly he makes a mistake! A hum comes out of him. He dowses it instantly. And looks round to see if I've heard. I have. His shirt and dinner-jacket creak and rustle apologetically. He looks at his watch.

"Well, if you're ready ..."

Of course I'm not ready. Let's see how badly he'll wait for me. And he *hates* being late for an opera.

Silver-kid gloves make you look like a surgeon operating on something in a space-ship, so I pick up the black doeskins which fit so tightly it's like being held by a little black hand when you have them on. What else for the funeral? My black satin Italian bag, almost too small for a lipstick the size of a torpedo, a bottle of scent (don't underestimate me, old Bloater), a white lace handkerchief from Switzerland with my initials embroidered on it by Swiss nuns (shame on you, Carlos, have you no decency? *Nuns*), my glasses for seeing all the faces on the stage (I put them on discreetly when the lights go down), my compact which has to be filled by a teaspoon dipping into my great box of banana-pink powder, my comb made of shiny aluminium like a dog's, no money (I shall borrow from the B. It's my duty to fleece him) and that seems to be the lot. No—safety pins, and nailclippers for my nails during the car ride, and front-door key, and rings—one to go over my glove. Now my fur coat. It's raccoon. George gave it to me last Christmas, and I've cut a lump out of the middle and belted it.

The creaking tolerance noises in the hall downstairs are coming up to a crescendo. Ah—my fan! I nearly forgot it. When I go down there are large oblong drops of sweat on the B.'s face, like raindrops on a Daimler. I say prettily:

"But we've got masses of time."

"We'll just make it if the traffic is all right."

As this is the way I normally do things, I'm not a bit put out, and sink comfortably into my seat.

With a big rev-up of the engine the B. drives us away in his '57 Cadillac. A bit of a let-down, but the B. never spends money on something that does not relate to his body. And he's constructed physically on too large a scale to need a motor-car for sex advertising and body-beautiful allure. This car is noisy but has vintage rating. I must say London looks quite different out of its windows. Again, just like St Petersburg with lots of sparkling lights as white as stars, and foreign-looking trees (oh, Billy) outlined down to the last twig by the glow of theatreland in front of us.

We rattle along, while I finish myself off, bearing in mind that the B. is staring fixedly through the windscreen. He's not looking at the traffic but streets and streets ahead where he can just see—if he narrows down his lids, which he does—the curtain going up. That makes him accelerate even faster. He's got his lips pinched together like an academic, or an old lady, crinkled up against one another rather unpleasantly. I hope he un-crinkles them before we go in.

I set to work with the furious energy of Cellini casting Perseus in bronze, finishing the work to the last detail, as he did, down to the celebrated toe of the godling. My hair has already been fixed unalterably in position; it's arranged in thickly gilded pieces. Damn, every time I try to do something detailed in the mirror we're certain to pull up suddenly at a traffic light and I freeze frigid like a rabbit while the other cars close in around us. Have you ever noticed that windows on motor cars are placed at every conceivable level? And when they stop and faces look out of them, it's like up-and-down tenement windows in some Limehouse laundry area backing onto a railway. I half expect to see a line of washing across a window or a budgerigar cage, with a fierce, energetic yellow bird looking at itself in a splashed mirror.

There's some rich evening air rushing by outside. I lower the window and I stick my nose into it: first-class quality. The B. instantly shivers; the poor hothouse plant.

"You'd better wear your gloves, Carlos. You're bound to get cold at the controls." *At the controls*, a rather leaden sarcasm but it has quality; most men would feel faintly ridiculous if you said it to them.

The B.'s reply is predictable.

"Thanks ... you may be right." He gets into his gloves reasonably well and fast while driving, though. One forgets he's quite a good pianist. He's probably got horribly nimble fingers.

"By the way, there's some terrine in the front locker, Min, if you're feeling hungry."

Hullo ... what's this? Has he got second sight? I must say he's determined to please tonight. Perhaps that dirty envelope said more than I thought it did. If he was able to decipher the love message which ran between the lines, it read: "Dear Lousy, if you're hoping to make me tight you can stew in your own juice, yours, Little Nell." (As usual I've paraphrased it a bit, but the gist was unmistakable). Hmm. He's paying me back in my own coin. I wouldn't put it past him to have a suckling-pig delivered to him in the foyer tonight. If so, I shall ask for pineapple.

I open the locker. Yes, there's a slice of terrine lying in its greased paper on a white cardboard plate. Hooray! I bite into it carefully, trying not to injure the double painting I've put on my mouth. I develop a frozen pout inside which I take in and swallow rapidly the arrogant, hybrid jelly-meat with its mongrel colours.

The time-lag between the accelerating car and the beginning of the performance is diminishing with every dark block of buildings we whistle through. We can both of us hear in our imaginations beautiful fat singers in their dressing-rooms letting out trills from their strong throats. Poor Bloater, how I have inhibited you! But for me, you'd be growling resonantly yourself. And the scenery, that's being glided into position with soft bumps; while light bulbs are switched on and off. But so long as the bassoons aren't already in the orchestra pit running up and down the scale, we're safe.

The Bloater swears and grinds his gears. Ah, parking! The graveyard of so many good evenings.

He rustily backs in with much twisting of neck-flesh ("We can't all be as hard as tennis-balls"). Then, with a final shudder, we're at rest. No wonder they talk about being a "motorist" these days, naming it as a profession. I always feel like a reincarnationist going quickly through a second life after forty minutes in a strange motor-car.

I get out, expatriated from the domestic motor-car into the dangerous, chill road. I feel as vulnerable as a newly-hatched butterfly with the scent still drying on my neck.

The B. bowls us along inside his opera cloak, and here we are—arrived. Gosh, what delicious stuffiness. The Turkey carpets are covered with freshly-washed people milling to and fro. You could be at the Bourse. I like these St John's ambulance nurses; with their elbowing manners and tom-boy heartiness they knock us all about, unable to wait for corpses. Also that antiseptic linen headgear they have on lends an almost indefinable astringent to the olfactory spectrum of odours which belongs to an expensive opera-house. A lot of musty dehydrated furs here tonight, at shoulder level it's like a ranch of petrified foxes. What loud sentences the middle classes exchange when they meet; are they shouting across one of Daddy's acres? Others say nothing, they just move inexorably in pairs, staring ahead and respirating through open mouths. Thank God for the continental thrusters; both sexes are here in numbers, as ugly as sin and most acceptable. You can always tell the Wagnerians, even on a Verdi evening; both men and women seem to be plastered with blue eye-shadow; they swarm through the porticos with mad eyes, they've lived longer, have more terrible opinions, and are definitely uglier than all the rest put together.

The Bloater is in his element. He knows *everyone*. People bow and scrape. He goes through all his rôles, according to whom we meet. His German and Italian are fluent. And he's not even showing off. A student with a baby face says about some future performance:

"I don't care. I'll be here anyway, Carlos. Even if it's only Amy singing Wotan!"

We go slowly upstairs to the crush bar where the smart set, with that special brand of dirty good looks which comes from irregular hours and unaired bedrooms, is drift-ing along with a melancholy glamour derived from a life divided between the mascara and drug counters in a chem-ist's shop. The escorts all have heads like brown, varnished doorknobs.

Just a minute, what have I done? A champagne cocktail has vanished down my throat, and I've got no record of it.

I feel as though I've swallowed splintered glass. We're at the centre of a pleasantly affected group, everyone talks sense loudly. I'm perfectly certain it's the best blah in the house at the moment, but I'm disturbed to find myself a little unsteady. I feel resentful towards Billy; why isn't he here? Bells ring and we go in to our seats.

From the front of the grand tier you can see nearly everyone in the house. The B. seats himself beside me and then looks at me. In his hand are a pair of opera glasses which he's offering to me. I'm suddenly aware that his eyes are kind, that he's eager, sensitive and much more than clever, brilliant. I'm hit by remorse. I've spent two years being offensive to this man. In return, he's done me nothing but good. He may even love me, in addition to being in love with me. In that case, it's serious, and I must behave seriously.

"Carlos …" It's almost the first gentle sound I've ever made for him.

He takes my hand, touches it with understanding, slithering his fingers over my knuckles for an instant, and then returns it to my lap again. My impulse is to get up and go straight home.

The lights are put out. And that enormous red and gold curtain, all fringes and tassels, and heavier than twenty lions dipped in blood, is rolled away.

Zut! There's the Garter Inn—we're right in the middle of the goings-on. People throw things and sing gaily. The lion-head beside me is still. He is smiling slightly. I sigh, and prepare to enjoy myself.

It's all right of course until you get the love-duet, *Labbra de foco!*, and then I can hardly bear to listen. To listen to an opera in the company of a man you are *not* in love with will only plunge you far more deeply into the power of the absent one. In fact, this is going on all over the opera-house. Everyone is in love with someone else. If you could see the yearning expressions or hear the desolate, solitary thunder of the corseted bodies!

I'm captivated, enchanted. My soul rips herself to pieces and by the first interval is whining for more champagne like an overheated violin. The B., much moved himself, leads us off to the little table just by the staircase where two gilt *tête-à-tête* chairs are propped inwards. Champagne and bucket, too.

Smoked salmon. I groan; and eat it. All I want to do is to get drunk and look for Billy. I feel a dark horse, like Racquel. At the thought of this name some strange premonition makes me raise my eyes.

Absolutely—of course. You've guessed correctly. There she is, in the middle of that animated throng, as pretty as ever I've seen her, in a sort of sari affair wound round her as usual (I mean just like those famous blouses) to show off her capable bosom. But *with* her? I'm straining every sinew. It must be, is it? That very handsome Indian, with the jet-black coat buttoned up under his chin. Oh, but he is distinctly the incarnation of Krishna, so distant, so jade-cold.

I wouldn't dream of mentioning it to the Bloater. Let him find out in his own good time. You can't hide anybody in an opera-house. They've probably got Billy down in the orchestra pits for all I know.

Oh God, everybody's here tonight. Where's George? And Claudi? Then we can all change partners and do a gavotte.

Racquel is coming up. The little beast. And leading that Indian like a haughty carving in chains. When I think of Jenny and myself, with our scholarly textual knowledge of Indian culture, right down to the unpronounceable sound "Sût," I could weep. I bet he's called Ram.

Racquel introduces him. For the first time in my life I feel that the whole bar *is* watching; I'm caught in a pincer movement between Bloaters and Rams and successful, radiant ginger women. Oh hell!

I'm glad to get back to my seat, but at once start hunting among the faces below me for familiar ones. (Billy.)

It's only at the end of the second act that I begin to come to myself. There's something about the Mistress Quickly scene which is familiar. The love-making, the hiding behind screens, the bursting in, the concealing of Falstaff in a laundry basket. Got it! It's Claudi and his MacFisheries routine with the Bloater all over again! I start to laugh. I can't help it.

By the second interval I'm in much better repair. The B. is at his most magnificent. There are women there who just can't take their eyes off him. With his cloak looped casually over the back of the little gilded chair, the clinking of our constantly raised glasses and our practised, non-stop eating in public and snapped-out repartee (mine) we have the formal shimmer and authority of a really successful religion.

I've begun to sparkle ever since I saw (in my mind) the B. getting into that laundry basket on the stage, with Claudi gleefully cramming down the lid on him. ("And I come round in a striped apron and hit him over the head with a fishmonger's cudgel.") I say aloud:

"Have you ever done the laundry-basket scene?"

He quaffs, pauses, puts a napkin across his mouth (I wonder he doesn't take a sitz bath before answering too) and replies:

"Many times. And you know going down in that chute from the window off-stage at the back really shakes you up if they're not careful. I remember once I got my neck jolted, and had to have massage for six weeks."

III

"Does the dirty linen affect your sinuses?" (Couldn't resist it.)

"Not terribly." He raises his head and thinks it over. He knows quite well what I'm up to, and won't play. He's got the end of the evening too well in mind to slip up now. He turns his head away so that his libertine's eyes go on looking at me out of their very corners, gleaming.

Racquel cuts our vision obliquely and disappears again. I suddenly feel my dress isn't low enough. Thought is catching, and the B. says:

"I must say your girl friend ... knows how to wear a sari. Not many European women ..."

It's fantastic the pure corn the Bloater will come out with. I, alone, must have heard that remark about two hundred times, and those who have lived longer will have an even better score. Even more fantastic, it works! I bridle up exactly as he intended:

"Oh crikey, don't give me that handsome woman-in-a-sari jabber. It doesn't go with the champagne. The best thing about that couple," I lean across the table, "is the man. He's got the oval eyes of the perfect lover."

I made that up on the spur of the moment, but it has an electric effect. The B. obviously thinks I know everything. I feel the brothel walls closing in as he says at once (*at once* mind you):

"So you fancy east of Suez love?"

Gosh. What next? I feel I'm getting into deep trouble. I play for time by splashing with my spoon into my fruit salad. East of Suez love indeed, what the devil does that mean? Something pretty murky; chop-sticks and long jump.

I decide not to answer. I make disdainful lips over the new bottle of champagne, remembering Billy's comment on bad champagne: "Bottled washing-up water from the continent."

The B. hangs on and on with his look, and gets nothing.

Eventually, I decide on a good sentence which should swing the balance of power towards me a bit. I say in the high tin of my English voice:

"It's just that he has a kind of smash-hit masculine beauty. I know a girl" (Jenny) "whose nose always runs when she's introduced to an attractive man. And all Indians are good at games, Carlos."

Worm your way out of that one if you can, Signor Driving-Gloves! The B. lets this drift out of his mouth:

"But they don't all hold the Black Belt."

"The Black Belt for Judo? Well, do you?"

"Ummmm" (muffled) "yes."

That's done it. He *is* as hard as tennis-balls. Claudi and I will have to go back to Square One in our Monopoly game *and* give up our "get out of jail" cards.

I look at him with extreme disfavour. It really is infuriating. I can't find anything wrong with him. And I just don't like him. I say tartly:

"Do you think I like you, Carlos?"

He hesitates, and answers carefully:

"I don't think that matters. I think you need me very, very badly."

I'm radiantly white with rage, and sit bolt upright staring at him with vixen's eyes. Clever, clever Bloater. I say:

"In what especial capacity?" (I must be off my head.)

Now's his chance to frame some piffling speech, something really scummy which will touch my heart made of pressed steel. The B. ignores the danger, gets up as the bells for the last act ring, and comes round to pull my chair back. These superb good manners are strictly for public consumption; in private he wouldn't even tie the shoelace of a woman's shoe or hand her the sugar for her tea. He says calmly:

"I think you need me badly in a sexual capacity."

He stands over me in a posture of pitiless, exultant ecstasy, as high and tilted as a steaming Wagon-Lit leaning over you in the Gare de Lyon on a winter's night.

If I could scorch the facing off his lapels with my eyes, I would.

Still, at least I can tell myself I'm part of life after all. But am I old enough, too old, to play this game?

That's the last time we speak before the "Bravos" and the final curtain. Do you realise he's only said "ummm" once this evening?

"I said: 'If you touch me I'll scream the house down.'"

"How *vieux jeu.*" That's Jenny.

"The man's old-fashioned. You've got to use old-fashioned phrases. Besides, it's an old-fashioned situation."

"Yes, but his behaviour is right up to date."

"Well, he didn't say a word in reply. He just started stripping off his clothes as if he was in his own bedroom. And laying out his money and his watch and so on, on the table. Very insulting."

"What on earth did you do?"

"George was asleep upstairs, so I danced about making shushing noises."

"I don't think you're any better at coping with sex-maniacs than I am, Min."

"I didn't know he was one until he got down to his shirt and trousers—you know what he did when I shushed him? He nodded and took his shoes off!"

"Oh, he's got no style."

"And then his shirt!"

"No! Couldn't you stop him?"

"Stop him? I didn't want to go anywhere near him. I didn't even want to be in the same country with him."

"How did he look with his shirt off?"

"Terrifying! He was wearing a satin cummerbund."

"Ugh! That's probably his black belt."

"He's got slabs and slabs of platinum-blond skin. It just filled the sitting-room. You couldn't get away from it."

"Honestly. They've got no shame."

"I was standing staring at it in horror. Then he lit a cigarette, as cool as a cucumber, and said: 'Let me make love to you. I'm good at it.'"

"That's rather disarming."

"Not when you're in love with someone else."

"So what did you do?"

"I'll tell you. I struggled decently. And then, every now and then, I thought: 'Yes, but this is the way out of Billy's power,' and I relaxed for a minute."

"That's fatal!"

"None of this would have happened if it hadn't been for Racquel!"

"Pooh. Of course it would. You must admit he attracts you a little."

I stop, and think. Then I say truthfully:

"It's the sort of attraction I don't want to respond to. It's all black. It's got no white in it."

"I know what you mean." Jenny knows very well what I mean.

"It's all right when I don't think."

"And *you* did think?"

"I tried not to. I thought instead how strong, clever, extraordinary, and adoring he was. That lasted for about four minutes."

"You can go a long way in four minutes," says Jenny, like everyone else we are not above the corny joke. I can hear that she's smiling from her voice at the end of the phone.

"Yes, well after the run I wanted to stop."

"And he wouldn't?"

"Have you ever tried to stop a steam-roller, all hissing with steam, or a bullock in the act of charging?"

"No."

"Neither had I until last night. I spat into his ear 'George will kill you' and it didn't have the slightest effect. Then I collected all my wits and said into the same ear in a very icy way, accenting each word: *'I don't like your smell.'*"

"Did it work?"

"It was like the hydrogen bomb."

"I must say it would have smashed me up. Did he come round?"

"No. That's the point. He let go. He looked at me. He thought about it. Then he sat down and scratched his head a bit. He didn't move for some time, and do you know, Jenny, I actually think he was reading a magazine on the floor beside him! Then he began very, very slowly to put on his shoes, lacing them up with extreme care. But the frightening thing was his expression."

"How was it?"

"Nothing there. Just a blank, scorched earth, you know, the steppes of Russia."

"How dispiriting. When you've smashed their masculine vanity, they always put on that sub-human Martian face, and look into space."

"I've never seen it before. It was like a great big empty rice pudding. I felt terrible."

"That's why they do it. To make you feel terrible."

"Was I utterly vile?"

"Not in the least. He brewed the whole thing up, all on his own. And think what fun he had undressing! That's quite enough for one evening."

"And I saw him in his cummerbund."

"Exactly. You saw him in his cummerbund, which was what he wanted. It's like seeing children in their bath."

"And I *didn't* call him 'Fatty.'"

"So you've got nothing to reproach yourself with."

"All the same I felt as mean as hell. I thought I ought to cook him something."

"No, you only cook them something when you tell them they *stink*, like Dr Johnson."

"Nothing for 'smell'?"

"Not even an egg and cress sandwich, toasted. Otherwise you'll be feeding half London."

"These ethics, Jenny, are so ... farcical!"

"I know, but the funny thing is, that's how you feel at the time!"

We've started to joke, but last night is still hanging over me. I say miserably:

"It really was a fearful *dénouement*. After all the pomp and ceremony, the score, the terrine, the red rose, and a really colossal drunkenness when we came out of *Falstaff* ... you know, I think if he'd kept his clothes on I wouldn't be talking to you now."

"You mean if he'd undressed *you*, and kept his cloak on ...?"

"And the purple tie and purple handkerchief. The lot."

"Manet had the right idea in *Déjeuner sur l'herbe*. Send the Bloater a print of it, with '*keep your shirt on*' written on the back!"

"Funny."

"No, Min, I do agree. A woman likes to be naked, or half-naked *first*. Definitely. Or else he should have got you in a hammer-lock you couldn't get out of."

"Oh Jenny, I don't necessarily mean *that*. You're so detailed and graphic."

"Min, but for me you'd never *live*. You're an absolute worm."

"I'm not an absolute worm. And is it 'living' to see an old

friend's stomach for the first time at the end of a long and tiring evening! It's a shock, I can tell you. Once I'd seen it, I kept getting pictures of the two of us in unpronounceable positions, up hill and down dale."

"Oh, you must never do that! You simply must concentrate on what you're doing."

"I wasn't doing anything."

"And don't grumble about stomachs. All you've seen is an upper stomach. Just wait till you see an upper and a lower together."

"The really curious thing is that I'm still fond of him, just as I used to be, while finding him unbearable ..."

"You're still fond of him, and definitely attracted, and you can't bear him. How simple. You know of course that a man can stand anything in sex *except* a woman who shoots him down in cold blood and goes on being fond of him?"

"Hmm. I don't care about that. It's the way I did it. I don't like myself very much. I once said to Billy, my musicologist: 'Who are the people you don't like, Billy?' and he said: 'People who are foul over the major things in life.'"

"I don't see what else you could have done."

"Well, I could have talked to you without making fun of him."

"What a waste! Besides it wasn't major. Major is babies and suicide."

"It's major when a man is over six foot. He's much more dangerous."

"By the way, Min, talking of danger, tell me *all* about Racquel and her Indian."

"She's got him on a lead, he's perfection. All this time, without a word to anyone, she's been having a well-managed, silent, successful, sex love-affair. You can see it written all over her … you know, her shoulders are free. No wonder she doesn't mind giving up an evening to go to a lecture at the Ethical Union!"

"While I have to sit by a telephone that doesn't ring when it should!"

I'm upset to hear the great Jenny close to tears.

"Oh Jenny, please give him up."

Silence.

"You're surely not going to let yourself be trapped by somebody's body? You who've slain so many?"

Moan, and swallow.

"What about the fascinating middle-aged man who said he was psychic?"

"I want my guitar, and I want him now."

"Cheer up. Sooner or later he'll bring out his dancing routine. And the scales will fall from your eyes."

When Fritz is taking his English examinations we all have to ask one another trick questions. For example, while he's carrying the washed milk bottles to the back door, he'll say: "Now you must think of a word like 'weighed' and put it in a different sentence."

"You mean a word you pronounce the same way?"

"Yes."

"Umm. (It's catching!) May I wade through the sea in my boots?"

"Ah! That's a nasty one." He shakes his head, thoroughly tricked, and chimes the bottles.

"Are you going to polish the sitting-room floor today?"

"Yes, I have just done it. Look there, there, there. That's not bad."

"And what about under things, Fritz? Did you go under that chest? What happens if people look there?"

"Listen, if they look there they will get hits."

The people who will get hits from Fritz are mounting up. Most women, all religious people ("Listen, they will get hits, the prayers."), those who look under chests, and now everyone on the board of examiners who asks him a trick question.

Actually Fritz is simplifying the language into a new kind of Esperanto. If someone comes to the door and he has to announce them, he calls upstairs simply:

"Mrs Min. Here is."

On the whole we play house very well together, although I get fed up when he keeps saying: "Vot shall I do now?" My mind goes blank, and we just stand there staring at one another hopelessly. I know that one of my weaknesses is the fact that I can't see dust. Either you have an eye for it or you haven't. I've been taught to see the fish lying in a stream, which means that I can penetrate through the glass clothes of a river and see its insides. Also I can tell when I'm halfway up a strange staircase whether the painting on the landing is going to be any good simply by the way the staircarpet has been attached to the stairs ... Oh, and the conversation of my host. But dust, not so easily. George, on the other hand, can find dust when there isn't any. He just lifts up a pot, looks round the hole, and says: "Dusty." His greatest happiness is writing his name in it. I suppose it's a more mature alternative to carving up park seats. He says the whole of London is dusty, and I answer: "Yes, but we can't get Fritz to dust the whole thing at seven shillings an hour."

Sometimes when I'm looking for dust, Fritz comes and says lugubriously:

"You know that Goethe says every man is a criminal after forty."

"Well, don't tell me, Fritz. I'm not forty and neither are you."

"Yes, but we have only a few more years to go, you know."

"Well, buck up and find some dust meanwhile. And then you can have all the fun of being a criminal to look forward to."

He glances out of the window at the golden-brown day and cheers up with a good idea:

"Shall I go and rake up the leaves?"

I immediately look out at the golden-brown day and want to do the same. Still, he had the idea first.

"All right. But please don't be greedy; leave me some. You can do two-thirds."

"Listen, it is not good for a woman to use a rake, I'm telling you."

"Gosh, forty already! You don't look it, either. If you're mean with the leaves I shan't ask you trick questions."

He goes out into the fresh air, grumbling happily. No wonder he's happy, the weather is so exciting in England. The different varieties of rain we get, everything from drifting muslin right through to drops of blood and bricks that fall from a roaring sky; and then there's the silent weather when nothing outside dares to move or cough, and the white-edged weather which is a prelude to the blue crumb of frost. People who want to get rid of their souls are always rushing out into the open air.

I've got soul trouble today, entirely due to my two Bs. And I keep asking myself: *"Am* I an absolute worm?" Surely, if I'm so wormlike they wouldn't have sacked me from school? I once told Jenny about it and she said:

"But what were you expelled for?"

"Reforming the syllabus. Stealing tomatoes. Gang warfare. Just nothing."

"Oh, that's no good. You've got to be expelled for syphilis or being a Lesbian. If possible, both."

I tried to think of something which would win me back a little lost ground.

"When it came to confirmation classes, they refused to confirm me."

"Why?"

"They said I wasn't 'ready.'"

"Huh! That only meant you hadn't developed sexually. Honestly schoolmistresses are a dirty bunch."

This sort of thing can lower your morale for months.

I decide to go upstairs and rummage through an old drawer of baby photographs to work out what level of wickedness I achieved in the past. My idea of myself has been cloudy ever since the Bloater undressed. In no time I'm absorbed in myself. There I am! What an excellent child, not especially intelligent or pretty, but me. I'm nearly always at the seaside it seems. And here are some old letters written by my grandmother to the headmistress, they're all about unaired beds. What curiosities! Yes, I remember now, everyone in England had an airing cupboard in which they used to air things. Extraordinary practice! I've never aired anything in my life, and I'm perfectly fit. But here's my grandmother sternly warning my boarding school that if they didn't air my bed, my vests, my blouses, and my pyjamas, I would never reach the age of seven.

Oh, Billy, I'm *not* a worm. How can I be when all I want to do is to go to bed with you? (aired or unaired).

Plim-Plam comes upstairs with its tongue out again. A minute later I hear Claudi hulloing from the front door, all ready to rush after it, and put it in.

"Are you there, my dear?"

"Yes, Claudi. You can come up and look at my baby photographs."

Claudi, who is thirsting for his story, is taken by surprise. He bides his time with a bad grace.

"Here I am, newly born."

"Your mother looks pretty."

"That's not my mother. That's my nurse."

"Well then, she looks pretty."

"Here I am at four."

"You haven't changed much. You've got exactly the same expression on your face, I've seen it dozens of times, whenever you've got a new man in your mind you make that Athena-the-bright-eyed face."

"I don't!"

"Sweetie-pie, you've got it on right now!"

So Billy is showing.

"Claudi, please, tell me truly. It's important. Am I a worm where men are concerned?"

"Aha! I knew it." He gets ferociously excited. "You ran away from him!"

"Interfering know-all!"

"She ran away! My little Min ran as fast as her legs could carry her!"

I've never seen him so jolly, it's nauseating. There's Fritz in the garden, cheerfully raking up all the leaves I want to rake up. And here's Claudi exploding with joy because he thinks I'm a worm. I say in a cross voice:

"You can take your pussycat and go, Claudi."

"Now, Min, Min, Min. What have we here? The same little girl with gout, except that she hasn't got gout any longer. But she's behaving as though she had."

"You didn't look at my baby photographs for more than a second."

"Oh how crafty! That isn't what made you angry, so don't pretend. You're angry because I've told you the truth about yourself."

It's true, I couldn't be angrier if I tried. I fold my arms just as Claudi did the other day, and borrow his useful legal manner:

"Are you talking about my ex-passion?"

"Aha! Out in the open, is it? So he's *ex* already. Really Min, the rate you get through them. But I knew it wouldn't work, my dear, because you're just like me, you hate opera—"

"You're mad, Claudi, it's one of my reasons for living."

"That's what you pretend. But I know you too well. No, my dear, I'm afraid you're made exactly like me. How many times have I sat through those dreadful Sphinxes in *Aida* with their dreadful folded-up headdresses, like trained nurses! No, I don't know which is worse, the opera or the ballet. In an opera people stop in the middle of dying, just when you think you're getting rid of them, and give a long explanation of what they're doing in Covent Garden Italian. In the ballet they come to the edge of the stage and dance like mad and never get anywhere; he throws her up with a gigantic effort to get rid of her, and she tries and tries to go, and they're still there at the end of the evening. It's the most frustrating thing I've ever seen."

At that moment there's a really uncivil knock on the front door, exactly like a furniture van backing into it. Claudi and I jump like guilty partners. We hurry downstairs, and when I open the door—expecting the B., or Racquel covered with half-moon shaped clawmarks, or George wanting his tea, or ... Billy—there's Claudi's double, the art dealer again. We goggle at him. But he, still simmering from that careless piece of haughtiness of mine, is fully in control and snaps:

"I think you have a painting which I brought at the request of Mr Carlos Hamburger?"

I instinctively look at my hands where most of the painting went. And then down to the corner beside the umbrellas where it's lying, still propped against the wall.

Again with a single gymnastic movement Claudi's double seems to dive in past our legs, and has seized the painting. He cries triumphantly:

"There it is. Thank you, Mrs So-and-so."

I grow two inches, and plate my voice with ice:

"Would you like to tell me what is going on?"

"Certainly." He tries to get round me but I block him. "Mr Hamburger wasn't sure whether you would like the painting, so he arranged for you to have it on loan for a few days until you'd made up your mind about it."

"I see." I think rapidly. "Well, can I have a look at it to see what I've decided?"

No one can deny I've outpointed him there. He writhes slightly, with the painting pressed to his stomach.

"Well, if you haven't had time even to look at it—"

"Oh, I've had time." Gosh, I'm nasty, and loving it, but he deserves it. One minute he's forcing a painting on me, and the next—after I've carefully stored it and dried off the streak of tomato soup for him—he's snatching it away from me. Evidently it's his way of taking exercise, first he climbs, now he jumps. What he needs is a beach-ball to bounce against the walls of people's houses.

"In that case I'd better take it away."

"Well, I wouldn't necessarily have been as harsh as that …"

Everyone knows that to give a present and then take it away is the basest action known to human kind. But for the Bloater to take away a painting I haven't even had time to dislike! That is a blue chip Bloaterism even I wasn't prepared for.

Claudi can't keep out of it, and says, with the scarlet running under his side whiskers:

"Let him take it, Min. It's too sordid. A chap like that …"

I decide, too, that the only thing for it is to be stunned by the sheer sordidness as well. I'm glad Claudi used that word, because it's not always possible to put your finger on beastly words when you need them to set your mood.

Claudi's double is absolutely determined to be "tackled." He jumps to one side, and then to the other. He even bothers to back up against the wall as though getting out of range of a body blow. At last he exhausts himself, and makes a rush for the front door, having had a thoroughly enjoyable five minutes. He sprints off.

George is terrible. He's creating scene after scene. What has happened? I'm bewildered, and my ego falls down off her plinth. I try on new coats, I do my keep-fit exercises, I improvise with my tapes, I write up my diary ... and George goes on being unmanageable. Someone's got their claws into him.

One day I go up to him and say:

"I'm terribly sorry, I'm afraid I may have ruined your life."

"Oh—but then I must have ruined your life too."

Billy writes to me constantly, careful not to make the endearments too rich at the end—just yet. I write back, equally careful, smiling as I do so. The way we begin and end letters is so indicative; it contains the essence of the fashions in culture and love of each generation. My grandfather used to write to my grandmother "My dearest wife" and sign off "your loving husband." That *was* mating.

Sometimes I make a list of all the bad things about Billy on a piece of paper, like a laundry list. He's not six foot, he's too ambitious, he never takes exercise, he's not well off, he's been divorced, he's ... perfect for me, and I know it. We meet but don't make love. Billy says:

"I'm desperate to make love to you."

Or he says:

"I want to make love to you three hundred times."

"What, only three hundred?"

Or it's I who begin such an exchange:

"Billy, do you think you could save your lust up for two months? Will it last that long?"

"Yes, it'll last about thirty years."

His verbal boldness astounds me; but is he saying phrases he's accustomed to? They don't seem to have the necessary raw edges, and there's absolutely no clumsiness in the way he brings them out. And then, his sophistication has almost exactly the same vein of naïveté in it that mine has. Has he caught it from me? Or have I already caught it from him?

Meanwhile we talk about everything under the sun.

But the eternal question in my mind is the familiar one: if we make love to one another, which one of us will love more? Am I going to be trapped by extreme skill? And if, alternately, I am not trapped, shall I despise?

We talk about our relations:

"What are yours like, Min?"

"Terrible. And yours?"

"Mine are too nervous to finish a sentence. They all live in the country."

"Oh good, then you're at home with nervous people like myself."

"Yes, of course. I'm fond of your nerves. They amuse me, and I don't mind what they do next."

"But I'm *too* nervous."

"That's what nerves are for. To make you nervous."

"Yours don't."

"Oh, I've had all mine out."

At every minute we lose or gain, and again lose. Sometimes at the end of an evening I risk sitting on the sofa in Billy's flat. Then it's my turn to be bold.

"I want to feel your weight."

"Am I too heavy on you?"

Suddenly I make a movement underneath him, sinuous, nerve-racking, and dare-devil, calculated to provoke him. He catches his breath at this insulting change of mood, and I get exactly the flash of rage I want as I say:

"No, I think I can accommodate your weight perfectly well, you know." And then, suddenly afraid: "Don't make a cruel mouth."

"It's a cruel situation." (Oh, Billy.) He cancels it quickly. "No, it isn't." It is, and it isn't; we know what we want.

But all these things, especially when his control breaks for a second, tell me what I want to know about him. Still, the physical summary is only a hundredth part of what is going on between us. I've found out that I've only got to watch his mouth to know his physical mind. Did I mention before what a perfect mouth it is? It's the thing about Billy which one would never know until one had kissed him; then once you're initiated into Billy's world, newly kissed by him, you never want to go back into the boring world you used to live in. Look at that boring chair you once sat upon while working at electronic tapes, perfectly contented. Now, it's unthinkable. The only un-boring chairs are those in Billy's flat, park benches where we've stopped, fold-up seats in concert halls, banquettes in taxis where we've jolted about softly together. On the days when I think he's getting a bit mean with the kisses at the end of his letter—only six crosses to last until Thursday morning—I get a letter by second post with just one big cross in it. Very right and proper. So one day I thrive and sing. And the next I write out my last will and testament, leaving all my music, my piano, my records and my tape-recorder, to Claudi, my faithful friend. And the next I go to a party and flirt *hard* with the only reasonable man there, and then just as he's writing down my telephone number I tell him I'm leaving for Rome the following day for six months.

It's George's fault. It's Racquel's fault. It's *Billy's* fault. But most of all, it's Claudi's fault for making life so sexy and so funny. If Claudi gave up questioning me and imputing and engineering, I'd never have the sort of outrageous ideas I've been getting nowadays. Is Claudi saving me from being prissy? Or is the scarlet that runs up and down his cheeks a red ink barometer of scandalous loose living? ("Oh we know all about her morals," says Claudi; "mind you, I wouldn't mind having an easy going set of morals like that myself!")

Billy is only slightly anxious about George, whom he doesn't like very much. He says:

"Has George ever started throwing things?"

I'm amazed and answer:

"It's funny you should say that. Because I often feel he's on the point of throwing something."

"Men always throw things when they're not getting enough love-making."

"Gosh, Billy, the things you know."

"You know just as many things I don't. Besides, women throw them back when *they're* not getting enough either. In the case of either sex, each man and each woman must get the kind of love he or she needs. If they don't get down to the depth which is right for them, they simply start throwing things at the wrong man or woman. It can make them very ill."

"Shall we ever do it?"

"No, never."

"Why not?"

"Because my desire for you is so great."

"But … what about mine?"

"Yours grows out of mine, didn't you know? Mine is just a split second ahead."

That's what he thinks. But every day is a bit more serious. I think we shall have to go away together.

An astonishing thing is happening. *We are actually getting to know one another:* six months ago I would have said such a relationship was impossible. I remember saying contemptuously to Billy:

"Really, what *are* the use of these random conversations?"

"It's the only way I can get to know you, Min."

Yes, it's curious. Especially for me. People specialise in telling me I'm "difficult." Lots of George's friends at the Museum, men of about fifty-eight with black thickets in their nostrils, literally save this up as the only thing which will give them any pleasure over a winter weekend: "Now I'll just go round there for a cup of tea so that I can explain to Min what a difficult sort of woman she is." I think they're all mock Bloaters. Ah, but my Bloater was always streets ahead of that. The trouble with him was, in retrospect, simple: too much passion. He forced me to be more and more feminine. If I had realised it at the time I would have said to him: "I can't claw you enough—for *you.*"

But in the case of Billy and myself, without more than a few caresses, we're already far beyond that point. All the quantities were right, so that out of the lightest beginnings, drifting thoughts which revealed similarities of outlook, followed by touch, discriminating and cautious, we've built our passion gracefully. You wouldn't think something constructed out of such odds and ends could become white-hot. It's because Billy has wisdom, something which has nearly vanished from the modern world. Every time I see him I feel I am on the edge of mystery ... and life itself. There are some very powerful human beings about in London today (Billy is one of them) and they take a lot of knowing. He says the Americans try to make sex pay out more and more sex-money, like a one-armed bandit. Whereas it won't. If you're lucky it pays out love and mystery. It has a time-scale built on moods and goodness; it's this moral dimension people forget. If you grab it, or get mean, it turns to ashes. Billy says one has to be gay and in love with the work of love.

As for me, I stubbornly refuse to re-dream the good times. I'm able to put up with the present only by attaching it to the future.

Yes, we are going away. At last! Billy said:

"How shall we go?"

I answered without a second thought:

"The Rome Express!"

"Of course. How stupid of me. The night train out of Paris with that excellent menu, and those Wagon-Lits, each with its miniature boiler which has to be stoked up with real coke."

"We'll *share* a sleeper. It'll be flaming."

"We'll have one of those basins with a lid which you hook up. And brass pedals for hot and cold water."

"Don't forget the three-cornered wall cupboard with the flasks of water—there's one with a wooden lid on a chain."

"And if you drink any other water you die."

"We'll clean our teeth in Pernod. Who'd fly, when they can play at the 1920s? You can wear the most English of your suits, and take up well-bred attitudes when you see a Frenchman in a blazer."

"You must wear skinny things like a horrid little school-girl. And only smile in a brittle, private way at *me*."

"At last—I can have the bottom bunk because I'm a

woman! And I don't have to give it up to some ratty old she-devil I'm sharing with." (Actually I've had very decent women, but one always imagines a Medusa.)

"Certainly not!"

"And we won't help lost Americans this time."

"We'll be absolutely foul to them. We won't change their ten-franc notes or tell them when they go through the Simplon tunnel. When they listen in we'll talk about tennis and chess."

"Will you mend my zip if it comes off?"

"Naturally. I'll undress you especially to mend your zips."

"We won't write postcards. We'll walk to and fro looking glossy. It'll be *impossible* to impress us."

"We'll simply order things the whole time."

"A real holiday! Is it true? We'll be guilty."

"Oh yes. But I always feel guilty, even when I'm travelling alone, not in love with Min. Don't you?"

"Much guiltier. In fact I feel less guilty now than I've done for years. And it's nothing to do with George being in love with X. But—Billy, oh Billy ... will it have a happy ending?"

"Of course. I specialise in happy endings. And you'll be my bitch."

"Oh. I quite want to be in your power. But you don't want me to love you full-out, surely? You wouldn't ask that of your greatest enemy."

"Well, you can just love me a little to begin with. Until you get more used to it."

"It's dangerous."

"Terribly.'

New Directions Paperbooks—a partial listing

Kaouther Adimi, Our Riches
Adonis, Songs of Mihyar the Damascene
César Aira, Ghosts
  An Episode in the Life of a Landscape Painter
Will Alexander, Refractive Africa
Osama Alomar, The Teeth of the Comb
Guillaume Apollinaire, Selected Writings
Jessica Au, Cold Enough for Snow
Paul Auster, The Red Notebook
Ingeborg Bachmann, Malina
Honoré de Balzac, Colonel Chabert
Djuna Barnes, Nightwood
Charles Baudelaire, The Flowers of Evil*
Bei Dao, City Gate, Open Up
Mei-Mei Berssenbrugge, Empathy
Max Blecher, Adventures in Immediate Irreality
Roberto Bolaño, By Night in Chile
  Distant Star
Jorge Luis Borges, Labyrinths
  Seven Nights
Beatriz Bracher, Antonio
Coral Bracho, Firefly Under the Tongue*
Kamau Brathwaite, Ancestors
Basil Bunting, Complete Poems
Anne Carson, Glass, Irony & God
  Norma Jeane Baker of Troy
Horacio Castellanos Moya, Senselessness
Camilo José Cela, Mazurka for Two Dead Men
Louis-Ferdinand Céline
  Death on the Installment Plan
  Journey to the End of the Night
Rafael Chirbes, Cremation
Inger Christensen, alphabet
Julio Cortázar, Cronopios & Famas
Jonathan Creasy (ed.), Black Mountain Poems
Robert Creeley, If I Were Writing This
Guy Davenport, 7 Greeks
Amparo Davila, The Houseguest
Osamu Dazai, No Longer Human
  The Setting Sun
H.D., Selected Poems
Helen DeWitt, The Last Samurai
  Some Trick
Marcia Douglas
  The Marvellous Equations of the Dread
Daša Drndić, EEG
Robert Duncan, Selected Poems

Eça de Queirós, The Maias
William Empson, 7 Types of Ambiguity
Mathias Énard, Compass
Shusaku Endo, Deep River
Jenny Erpenbeck, The End of Days
  Go, Went, Gone
Lawrence Ferlinghetti
  A Coney Island of the Mind
Thalia Field, Personhood
F. Scott Fitzgerald, The Crack-Up
  On Booze
Emilio Fraia, Sevastopol
Jean Frémon, Now, Now, Louison
Rivka Galchen, Little Labors
Forrest Gander, Be With
Romain Gary, The Kites
Natalia Ginzburg, The Dry Heart
  Happiness, as Such
Henry Green, Concluding
Felisberto Hernández, Piano Stories
Hermann Hesse, Siddhartha
Takashi Hiraide, The Guest Cat
Yoel Hoffmann, Moods
Susan Howe, My Emily Dickinson
  Concordance
Bohumil Hrabal, I Served the King of England
Qurratulain Hyder, River of Fire
Sonallah Ibrahim, That Smell
Rachel Ingalls, Mrs. Caliban
Christopher Isherwood, The Berlin Stories
Fleur Jaeggy, Sweet Days of Discipline
Alfred Jarry, Ubu Roi
B.S. Johnson, House Mother Normal
James Joyce, Stephen Hero
Franz Kafka, Amerika: The Man Who Disappeared
Yasunari Kawabata, Dandelions
John Keene, Counternarratives
Heinrich von Kleist, Michael Kohlhaas
Alexander Kluge, Temple of the Scapegoat
Wolfgang Koeppen, Pigeons on the Grass
Taeko Kono, Toddler-Hunting
Laszlo Krasznahorkai, Satantango
  Seiobo There Below
Ryszard Krynicki, Magnetic Point
Eka Kurniawan, Beauty Is a Wound
Mme. de Lafayette, The Princess of Clèves
Lautréamont, Maldoror

Siegfried Lenz, The German Lesson
Alexander Lernet-Holenia, Count Luna
Denise Levertov, Selected Poems
Li Po, Selected Poems
Clarice Lispector, The Hour of the Star
    The Passion According to G. H.
Federico García Lorca, Selected Poems*
Nathaniel Mackey, Splay Anthem
Xavier de Maistre, Voyage Around My Room
Stéphane Mallarmé, Selected Poetry and Prose*
Javier Marías, Your Face Tomorrow (3 volumes)
Adam Mars-Jones, Box Hill
Bernadette Mayer, Midwinter Day
Carson McCullers, The Member of the Wedding
Fernando Melchor, Hurricane Season
Thomas Merton, New Seeds of Contemplation
    The Way of Chuang Tzu
Henri Michaux, A Barbarian in Asia
Dunya Mikhail, The Beekeeper
Henry Miller, The Colossus of Maroussi
    Big Sur & the Oranges of Hieronymus Bosch
Yukio Mishima, Confessions of a Mask
    Death in Midsummer
Eugenio Montale, Selected Poems*
Vladimir Nabokov, Laughter in the Dark
    Nikolai Gogol
Pablo Neruda, The Captain's Verses*
    Love Poems*
Charles Olson, Selected Writings
George Oppen, New Collected Poems
Wilfred Owen, Collected Poems
Hiroko Oyamada, The Hole
José Emilio Pacheco, Battles in the Desert
Michael Palmer, Little Elegies for Sister Satan
Nicanor Parra, Antipoems*
Boris Pasternak, Safe Conduct
Octavio Paz, Poems of Octavio Paz
Victor Pelevin, Omon Ra
Georges Perec, Ellis Island
Alejandra Pizarnik
    Extracting the Stone of Madness
Ezra Pound, The Cantos
    New Selected Poems and Translations
Raymond Queneau, Exercises in Style
Qian Zhongshu, Fortress Besieged
Herbert Read, The Green Child
Kenneth Rexroth, Selected Poems
Keith Ridgway, A Shock

Rainer Maria Rilke
    Poems from the Book of Hours
Arthur Rimbaud, Illuminations*
    A Season in Hell and The Drunken Boat*
Evelio Rosero, The Armies
Fran Ross, Oreo
Joseph Roth, The Emperor's Tomb
Raymond Roussel, Locus Solus
Ihara Saikaku, The Life of an Amorous Woman
Nathalie Sarraute, Tropisms
Jean-Paul Sartre, Nausea
Judith Schalansky, An Inventory of Losses
Delmore Schwartz
    In Dreams Begin Responsibilities
W. G. Sebald, The Emigrants
    The Rings of Saturn
Anne Serre, The Governesses
Patti Smith, Woolgathering
Stevie Smith, Best Poems
    Novel on Yellow Paper
Gary Snyder, Turtle Island
Dag Solstad, Professor Andersen's Night
Muriel Spark, The Driver's Seat
Maria Stepanova, In Memory of Memory
Wislawa Szymborska, How to Start Writing
Antonio Tabucchi, Pereira Maintains
Junichiro Tanizaki, The Maids
Yoko Tawada, The Emissary
    Memoirs of a Polar Bear
Dylan Thomas, A Child's Christmas in Wales
    Collected Poems
Tomas Tranströmer, The Great Enigma
Leonid Tsypkin, Summer in Baden-Baden
Tu Fu, Selected Poems
Paul Valéry, Selected Writings
Enrique Vila-Matas, Bartleby & Co.
Elio Vittorini, Conversations in Sicily
Rosmarie Waldrop, The Nick of Time
Robert Walser, The Assistant
    The Tanners
Eliot Weinberger, An Elemental Thing
    The Ghosts of Birds
Nathanael West, The Day of the Locust
    Miss Lonelyhearts
Tennessee Williams, The Glass Menagerie
    A Streetcar Named Desire
William Carlos Williams, Selected Poems
Louis Zukofsky, "A"

*BILINGUAL EDITION

For a complete listing, request a free catalog from New Directions, 80 8th Avenue, New York, NY 10011
or visit us online at ndbooks.com